Eric Sterling Secret Agent

Smugglers on Grizzly Mountain

ERNEST HERNDON

ZondervanPublishingHouse
Grand Rapids, Michigan

A Division of HarperCollins*Publishers*

Smugglers on Grizzly Mountain
Copyright © 1994 by Ernest Herndon

Requests for information should be addressed to:
Zondervan Publishing House
Grand Rapids, Michigan 49530

Library of Congress Cataloging-in-Publication Data

Herndon, Ernest.
    Smugglers on Grizzly Mountain / Ernest Herndon.
      p.   cm. (Eric Sterling, secret agent)
    Summary: Twelve-year-old Eric and his fellow wildlife conservation
agents must face harsh Alaskan weather, grizzly bears, and mushroom
smugglers.
    ISBN 0-310-38281-5 (paper)
    [1. Adventure and adventurers—Fiction. 2. Smuggling—Fiction.
3. Alaska—Fiction. 4. Grizzly bear—Fiction. 5. Bears—Fiction. 6. Wildlife
conservation—Fiction.]
I. Title. II. Series: Herndon, Ernest. Eric Sterling, secret agent.
PZ7.H43185Sm   1994
Fic—dc20   93-44161
                                                       CIP
                                                       AC

Edited by Dave Lambert
Cover design by Jim Connelly
Cover illustration by Jim Connelly
Internal illustrations by Craig Wilson, The Comark Group

Printed in the United States of America

94 95 96 97 98 99 /❖LP/ 10 9 8 7 6 5 4 3 2 1

For Robert, Dan, and Marvin

1

"Boy, have I got a surprise for you kids," Miss Spicc told us as we walked into her office at Wildlife Special Investigations headquarters.

"What is it?" asked Sharon.

"I mean, you're going to *love* this," said the tall, plump, pretty director of WSI as she motioned us toward three chairs near her desk.

"But what *is* it?" asked Erik K., Sharon's brother.

"Yeah, come on—tell us," I said, grinning in anticipation of the good news.

She lowered her voice. "We're going backpacking."

My grin disappeared. "Backpacking? Isn't that where you, like, put a heavy pack on your back and walk up mountains?"

"Hey, cool! That'll be a good workout," said thirteen-year-old Erik K., who has a black belt in karate and loves exercise.

"Maybe we'll see some wildlife!" said his twelve-year-old honey-blond sister, who's great with animals.

"Yeah, like snakes or bears," I said grimly. Sharon and I were the same age but we had different ideas about some things.

Miss Spice laughed. "Oh, Eric C., cheer up. You always start out complaining but then wind up enjoying your assignments."

Assignment! I knew there'd be a catch. As secret agents for WSI, Erik K., Sharon, and I often went on difficult, dangerous missions to protect wild animals. Miss Spice thought nothing of sending us to foreign countries or spooky swamps or remote islands.

"What kind of assignment is this?" I asked.

Miss Spice grinned and stood up. "You'll find out. But first let's go down to the supply room and get ready for our little trip."

"Where will we hike?" Sharon asked as we followed Miss Spice across a huge room full of men and women sitting at computers and telephones.

"Seven Falls Park," she said, leading us down a hall and through a door. She clicked on a light to reveal a large storage area full of every sort of outdoors equipment, all carefully sorted and organized. She selected backpacks, sleeping bags, tents, campstove, canteens—and a telescope.

"What's the telescope for?" Erik K. asked.

"Oh, I thought we'd do some stargazing tonight."

"Tonight?" I said. "You mean we're going now?"

"Sure. It's early. We have plenty of time to drive to the park and hike down the trail. And I've already cleared it with your parents."

"All right!" said Erik K., trying on a bright blue pack. "Hey, nothing to it."

"That's empty," I said. "Just wait till it has stuff in it."

Sharon, meanwhile, was fingering the telescope gently. "I've always wanted to look through one of these."

"Well, you'll get to do plenty of it," Miss Spice said. "Now, let me show you the proper way to pack a backpack."

"You're the outdoors type, aren't you, Miss Spice?" I said.

She tossed her ginger-colored hair proudly. "You bet! Backpacking, canoeing, horseback riding—I love it all."

"Why do you think they made her director of a wildlife agency, dufus?" Erik K. said.

"I just figured it was because she's so smart," I retorted.

Miss Spice ruffled my hair. "Oh, Eric C., you're such a sweetheart."

I stuck my tongue out at Erik K., who grinned.

"Now," said Miss Spice, "let's get down to business."

She had already bought food for the trip, so we divvied it up and filled our packs, with Miss Spice showing us how to center the load. When we had the packs filled and strapped tightly closed, she showed us how to adjust the shoulder straps and hip belt.

"Hey, this isn't so bad after all," I said, surprised at the way the weight rested on my hips rather than my shoulders. "I used my dad's old scout pack once, and it didn't feel anything like this."

"They've come a long way in making backpacks," Miss Spice said with a smile. She glanced at our feet. "We'll swing by your houses so you can get some boots or old tennis shoes, plus swimsuits, and jackets in case it gets chilly tonight."

Soon we and our gear were crowded into the WSI jeep, heading for Seven Falls Park. Several miles outside of town, Miss Spice pulled into the park entrance, registered at the check-in station, and drove down a winding road beneath tall trees, stopping at last in a small gravel parking lot.

"Here's the trailhead," she said as we got out.

"How far will we be hiking?" Sharon asked.

"We'll camp at the first waterfall, about a mile from here."

"Piece of cake," Erik K. said, pulling our equipment out of the jeep.

Strapping on our packs, we followed Miss Spice to the edge of the forest, where the trail started.

"Oh," she said, pausing. "I forgot to tell you. Be very careful where you put your feet. This place is crawling with snakes."

2

Crawling with snakes! Suddenly every leaf on the ground seemed to be moving as I imagined reptiles swarming under the leaves.

"Shouldn't we be carrying guns or something?" I asked.

Miss Spice laughed. "Don't worry, Eric C. They're more afraid of us than we are of them."

"Yeah," Sharon said, nodding. "They try to get away from people. There are lots of snakes in the woods, but you hardly ever see them because they hide from you."

I didn't feel very reassured, and I noticed Erik K. also watched where he put his feet down as we walked down the path. Miss Spice set a brisk pace, followed by Sharon, Erik K., and me. The trail went down a steep hill, then began to go up.

"Hey, this is a mountain," I called.

"Don't be silly," said Miss Spice, who didn't seem at all out of breath. "It's just a little hill."

A hill maybe—but hardly little. I was relieved when we made it to the top, but going down the other side wasn't much easier. It was tricky figuring out where to put my feet on the steep slope. Only when I reached the bottom did I realize I'd forgotten all about snakes.

We crossed two more hills before we reached a small, clear stream.

"This is Clay Creek," said Miss Spice.

The trail ran alongside the stream—downstream, I was glad to see, and not up. The stream made a perky, bubbling sound, but before long I heard a roaring noise up ahead. Erik K. turned and gave me a thumbs up. "Sounds like a waterfall."

Soon the trail opened out on a large area, obviously a campsite. A ring of stones surrounded a heap of ashes where other hikers had built campfires. Miss Spice stopped and removed her pack. "Here we are."

Erik K. quickly dropped his pack and dashed to the creek. I hurried after him. Our campsite was right at the top of the waterfall; the stream slid over a clay shelf and gushed over the dropoff in a thin plume.

"Must be twenty feet!" Erik K. said, gazing to the small pool below.

"Cool!" I said.

Sharon appeared beside us. "I like the way the water carves grooves in the clay," she said. "It makes chutes and tubes."

"Isn't this wonderful?" said Miss Spice, joining us.

"Yeah!" we chorused.

She put a hand on my shoulder. "Was it worth the effort, Eric C.?"

"You bet!"

"Let's eat a bite of lunch, then we'll explore."

"All right!" said Erik K., who was always hungry.

After a quick lunch we left our packs at the campsite and continued down the trail. The stream flowed around a bend and dropped down another fall.

"That's two!" Erik K. said.

Following the trail, we found more waterfalls, most of them small, until at last there was just one to go. Plodding up a tributary, Miss Spice paused and pointed. "Number seven."

Ahead of us, a waterfall rose thirty feet from the stream.

"That's the highest one yet!" Erik K. said as we scrambled toward it.

"Hey, here's a big pool!" Sharon said when she reached the base of the falls. "May we swim, Miss Spice?"

"Be my guest."

We'd worn our swimsuits under our clothes, so we undressed and waded in. Miss Spice perched on a rock in the sunshine.

"This is like ice!" I said.

"Boy, this clay is gooey between my toes," Erik said.

Sharon plunged in and came up with her hair streaming. "Brrr!"

Erik reached underwater and came up with a handful of clay. "It's nearly blue," he said, examining it. He painted two streaks across his face. "War paint." Then he grinned at his sister and grabbed another blob of clay.

Uh-oh. I knew from past experience how much Erik likes a mud fight.

"Erik K., you'd better not!" She raised her hands and backed away.

Her brother gave a whoop and hurled the stuff, which landed smack on her forehead. Sputtering, she washed her face off, then grabbed some ammunition of her own.

I knew it wouldn't be long before Erik would try to include me in the battle, and I didn't want to be an easy target. I swam across the pool to the curtain of water pattering down. Closing my eyes, I passed through it into the cool, shadowy hollow behind the falls. The rock wall curved under and formed a broad shelf.

Wiping the water from my eyes, I noticed a chunk of wood on the shelf. Then, as my eyes focused, I saw it wasn't wood at all. It was a snake, coiled up and testing the air with its forked tongue!

3

"Snake!" I screamed, plunging back into the pool.

I shot out onto the bank like a scared monkey, with Erik and Sharon not far behind. Miss Spice sat up in alarm.

"What? Where?" she demanded.

"Behind the falls! A big snake, coiled up!" I replied breathlessly.

"Poisonous or nonpoisonous?" Sharon asked.

"How should I know?"

Sharon frowned, studying the falls. "I bet if I went around the edge I could see it and tell."

"No, Sharon, you'd better not," Miss Spice said.

"Oh, please, Miss Spice. I handle my dad's snakes all the time." Dr. Stirling, Sharon's father, is a veterinarian for the city zoo, and he often brings sick animals home for treatment.

"Well, all right, but be very careful."

Sharon began picking her way around the edge of the pool.

"Look out!" Erik K. shouted, and Sharon jumped. "Oh," he said, "it's only a stick."

His sister glared at him. "You nearly gave me a heart attack."

"Sorry."

At last she reached the waterfall and stuck her head through the silvery curtain. A moment later she turned to us, smiling. "It's just a water snake! It's harmless!"

"I don't care. I'm not going back in," I said.

"Me neither," Erik K. said. "Might be some poisonous ones around."

Miss Spice checked her watch. "Actually, we should be getting back to camp. We need to pitch the tents, cook supper, and build a campfire."

"I'll build the fire!" Erik K. volunteered. "Okay, Miss Spice?"

"I don't see why not," she said, rising.

We dressed and returned to camp. Sharon, Miss Spice, and I pitched the two tents while Erik K. rustled up firewood. Then Miss Spice made supper on the campstove. By the time we finished eating, the sun was nearly down.

"Time to start the fire now, Miss Spice?" Erik K. asked.

She smiled. "Go ahead."

He already had a little heap of dry pinestraw in the center of the ring of stones, with twigs piled up like a tepee over it. He struck a match and slipped it under the pinestraw, which sent up a thick stream of yellow smoke. Then it poofed into flames, and Erik quickly added more twigs. He leaned over and blew on the blaze to make it burn higher. "A one-match fire," he bragged. "Am I a great woodsman, or what?" The rest of us grinned at each other and decided to ignore him.

"When are we going to use the telescope, Miss Spice?" Sharon asked.

Miss Spice smiled. "As soon as it's dark, honey."

"Can't you use it in the daytime, like to look at birds or animals?"

"As a matter of fact, you can. We couldn't see very far in these woods, though."

"Yeah, how are we going to see the stars through the trees?" Erik K. asked, stomping on a large stick to break it.

"If we put the telescope near the waterfall I think we'll have a good view."

"May we start now?" Sharon asked. "Maybe we can see some animals."

Miss Spice chuckled. "Oh, all right." Fetching the telescope case, she walked to the edge of the cliff near the waterfall. She set up the tripod and aimed the scope at the stream below.

"It's kind of blurry," Sharon said, peering into the lens.

Miss Spice nodded. "That's a high-powered telescope. It's designed for great distances. This is really too close for it."

Sharon aimed the scope up into the trees and adjusted the focus. "Hey, look! A cardinal!"

"Where? Let me see," I said.

She moved aside and I stared into the lens. Nothing but pine needles—the bird must have hopped away. After some searching, I found the bright red bird on a branch higher in the tree. It seemed so close I could see its yellow beak and blinking eyes. Its throat swelled and its beak opened, and I knew it must be chirping even though we couldn't hear it over the rush of the falls.

"How far away could you see with this telescope—on the ground, I mean?" Sharon asked.

"Oh, miles," Miss Spice said. Then she grinned. "In fact, you'll be using this telescope on your assignment."

Erik, who had built the fire up to his satisfaction, joined us. "What *is* our assignment?" he asked.

"Yeah," I said. "Tell us."

"Here's a hint: You three will be going to a place with glaciers and tundra."

"Canada?" Sharon guessed.

Miss Spice shook her head.

"Siberia!" said Erik K.

"Nope."

"Alaska?" I tried, and she nodded. "But Miss Spice! People freeze to death in Alaska!"

4

Erik and Sharon didn't seem bothered by the idea of going to Alaska, but I was so anxious about it that I couldn't concentrate on stargazing. I was glad when we finally finished and returned to the warmth of Erik's campfire. He added more sticks to the blaze, and we all sat cross-legged on the ground around it.

"Are you going to tell us the rest of our assignment now?" I asked.

Miss Spice laughed. "Don't sound so gloomy, Eric C. It's not as bad as all that."

"It is too! I don't know anything about survival in the frozen North."

"Shhh," Sharon said. "Let her tell."

"Well, have you ever heard of Denali?" Miss Spice began.

"Isn't that the new name for Mount McKinley?" Sharon said.

Miss Spice smiled. "Actually, that's the *old* name for Mount McKinley. The Indians called it Denali long before any pioneers came along."

"Isn't that like the biggest mountain in North America or something?" Erik K. asked.

"That's right. It's more than 20,000 feet high."

"Uh-oh," I said. "I get it. We're going to have to backpack up the mountain. That's why you've been showing us about backpacking."

"Not quite," Miss Spice said with a laugh. "Scaling Denali is a challenge even for expert mountain climbers. No, what I want you to do is hike up a much smaller mountain just outside Denali National Park. It's steep, but nothing like the big peak. In fact, it's less than 5,000 feet."

"That's almost a mile straight up!" I said.

"Don't worry," she said with a chuckle. "You'll have plenty of time to prepare."

"But what will we do there? What's the assignment?" Sharon asked.

"You'll hike up a trail onto Bear Ridge. There you'll make camp and set up an observation post with the telescope."

"You want us to look at stars in Alaska? Why?" Erik K. asked.

"Not stars," Miss Spice said. "Smugglers."

"Smugglers?" we chorused.

"Mushroom smugglers. You see, the lower slopes of Denali are covered with mushrooms and lichens. Unfortunately, there's a big market for them. Some mushrooms bring up to one hundred dollars apiece in Japan."

"Why would anybody pay a hundred dollars for a mushroom?" I asked.

"Well, they're delicious to eat, for one thing. Gourmet chefs especially like to use them. But whatever the reason, there's a big market for Alaskan mushrooms. Now, it's against the law to pick mushrooms in the national park, and until recently collectors stayed outside the park borders. But mushrooms are getting so scarce now that some of the collectors are moving into the park."

"Why don't the park rangers just arrest them?" Erik K. asked.

"For one thing, Denali National Park has six million acres. That's bigger than the state of Massachusetts," Miss Spice said. "There's no way rangers can patrol an area that size. Plus, the park rangers have a thousand other duties, like clearing trails and rescuing stranded mountain climbers. That's why they asked WSI to help."

"I don't understand," Sharon said. "I mean, I thought we were supposed to protect animals, not plants."

Miss Spice nodded, as if expecting the question. "Scientists say 95 percent of all plant life depends on fungi—you know, like mushrooms. A single mushroom might have miles of tiny little roots that draw nutrients to the surface, where other plants feed on them. So, what feeds on plants?"

"Animals!" Erik K. answered.

"Exactly. Think of all the creatures in Alaska that eat plants."

"Caribou," I said.

"Moose," added Erik K.

"Bighorn sheep," Sharon put in.

"And lots more," Miss Spice said. "So even though mushrooms and lichens seem unimportant, all kinds of things depend on them."

"So our assignment is to watch for smugglers through the telescope," Erik K. guessed.

Miss Spice nodded. "Rangers have found evidence that the smugglers are coming in from the southeast side of the park. What we need is somebody to watch that area. When you see the smugglers, you'll radio one of our agents below, and he'll alert the park rangers."

"Doesn't sound so hard," Erik K. said.

"It shouldn't be." She sighed. "I just wish there was some way to educate people so they wouldn't do these things to start with."

"How can you educate a crook?" I said skeptically.

"Isn't that what Christians are supposed to do?" Sharon said. "Get people to change their ways? I thought the whole story of the Bible was that bad people *can* become better."

"Why do we have jails, then? If you want to save wildlife, better catch the lawbreakers and throw 'em in jail, that's what I say," I said.

"I hope you're wrong, Eric C.," Miss Spice said softly.

"Well, what will the weather be like?" Sharon asked.

"Don't be dumb, sis," Erik K. said. "It's the middle of the summer."

Miss Spice smiled, "That's true, but where you're going it can snow even in the summer. That's not likely, but you can expect chilly, wet weather. I'll see to it that you have the proper equipment."

"Hey," I said. "I just thought of something else that eats plants—grizzly bears."

"Yes, and unfortunately this is the time of year when they're most active," Miss Spice said. "They're out eating berries and catching salmon. Our man in Alaska will explain how to stay safe from bears."

Even though the night was warm and the campfire crackled cozily, a shiver ran through my body as I pictured blizzards and attacking bears. I moved closer to the blaze.

5

Miss Spice gave us each a pair of hiking boots, and for the next several days we practiced hiking up and down the bleachers at the football field with loaded packs on. Not exactly my idea of a good time, but Miss Spice usually joined in. Even though she wasn't going to Alaska with us, she said she needed the exercise.

By the time we boarded the plane for Anchorage, Alaska, we were fed up with bleachers and anxious for the real thing. But it took a while—we'd been in the air for several hours when Erik K., who sat by the window, said, "Hey, look at this!"

Sharon and I leaned over to peer out. Far below stretched a rugged coastline of rocky mountains and smooth glaciers.

"Just think if we crashed here!" Erik K. said.

"Hush, Erik K.," Sharon chided. "We're not going to crash."

"We'd never get out alive, even if we survived the crash," I said.

"You two stop that!" Sharon said.

"Bet it's crawling with grizzly bears down there," Erik K. said, teasing his sister.

"I'm not afraid of a grizzly," she said.

"How do you know? Dad won't let you go near the ones at the zoo."

"That's just because they're too big to bring home when they're sick. I bet they can be gentle just like all the other animals Dad's cared for."

"Gentle to you, maybe," I said, remembering a lion Sharon helped nurse. "They'd probably eat me in one bite."

"You and me both!" Erik K. said, still scanning the rugged terrain below.

"Yeah, but you know karate," I reminded him.

"Karate? Against a thousand-pound grizzly bear? He'd swat me like a mosquito."

We got to Anchorage around nine at night, but the sun was still well up in the sky. That was no surprise. Miss Spice had explained that, in the summertime, the sun didn't set in Alaska till nearly midnight, and rose again just a few hours later.

We were surprised, though, by the scowling, dark-bearded man who met us in the airport. "So you're the wildlife kids, huh?" he muttered, raising one eyebrow. "I'm Martin Bull. Come on, let's get your luggage."

As we walked down the crowded corridor I heard him grumble, "Got to play babysitter ... bunch of kids ..."

We glanced at each other and shrugged. *What a grouch*, I thought.

Collecting our backpacks, we followed Mr. Bull outside to a van. He threw our packs into the back as we climbed in.

"You kids ever been to Alaska before?" he asked as he settled into the driver's seat. "Didn't think so. Hmmm ... Better off to stay home ... No place for kids ..."

He almost seemed to be talking to himself. His sentences trailed off as if he didn't care whether we heard him or not. "Call me up on some stupid assignment ... S'posed to be retired ... Got better things to do than ..."

As we drove through the city of Anchorage, I noticed tall, snow-capped mountains not far away. I still couldn't get over how bright it was this late.

Mr. Bull drove to a house in the suburbs. He parked in the driveway and we entered a huge garage lined with all sorts of fishing and camping equipment.

"Wow! You've got as much stuff as the WSI storeroom," Erik K. said.

"Ha—WSI storeroom? I should say so . . . Been camping all my life . . . You think I need a kid to tell me how much stuff I got? . . . Send a bunch of kids to Alaska . . . backcountry . . . grizzly bears all over the place . . ."

"Uh—did you say something about grizzly bears, Mr. Bull?" I asked.

"Grizzly bears? You bet I did . . . Denali's swarming with 'em . . . Wouldn't catch me out there without an Uzi . . . Crazy idea, sending kids to bear country . . ."

Erik K., Sharon, and I stared at each other, worried. What had Miss Spice gotten us into? Then Mr. Bull shoved open a door into a brightly-lit kitchen, and we hurried after him.

"Why, here they are!" said a short-haired, red-faced, smiling woman. "I'm Sharon Bull. So glad to see you children."

I felt so relieved to see a friendly face that I nearly hugged her.

"I'll bet you're starved," the woman said, quickly setting the table.

"Bunch of kids . . . Eat us out of house and home . . ." Mr. Bull muttered.

Mrs. Bull pecked him on the cheek. "Oh, hush, Marty. Can't you see these kids are homesick?"

He glanced at us and raised an eyebrow. "Homesick! Who's homesick?"

"Not me," Sharon piped.

28

"Me neither," Erik K. said.

"What about you?" Mr. Bull said to me. "You homesick?"

I shrugged and looked down.

"Ever fished for salmon, kid?"

"No sir."

"Hmm. Didn't think so . . . We're going down to Kenai tomorrow . . . Salmon running . . . Fishing oughta be good . . . You're here, might as well make the best of it . . ." He wandered off into the living room. "Wash my hands . . ."

Mrs. Bull gave us a smile. "Don't mind him," she told us. "He's thrilled to have you. He's been excited all week. He finally has someone to take fishing."

6

Next morning, Mr. Bull and the three of us left Anchorage in his van loaded with fishing gear. Mrs. Bull would have come, too, but it was hard for her to get time off from her job as a nurse at a hospital in Anchorage. We drove past ocean inlets, glaciers, mountains, forests, and rushing rivers. The country looked wild, but the highway was crammed with cars, trucks, vans, and RVs, many with license plates from other states.

"Crazy tourists," Mr. Bull muttered as we drove behind a slow-moving RV. "Clog up the highways, cause accidents ... Come up here and pollute our oxygen ... Oughta stay home, fish in their own waters ..."

"Why are there so many of them?" Erik K. asked.

"*Salmon*, boy, salmon. It's summer, sockeye are running . . . Rivers full of 'em . . . More fish than there are people, if you can believe it . . ."

It took several hours to reach the town of Soldotna on the Kenai River. Mr. Bull pulled into a campground full of RVs and tents. Fishermen lined the nearby river bank. Mr. Bull parked in front of a small camper-trailer.

"This is it . . . Home away from home, where I come to fish . . . Have to put up with all these crowds . . . Way it is if you want to catch sockeye . . . Come on, let's get our hooks in the water . . ."

Despite his perpetual frown, Mr. Bull did seem excited, as Mrs. Bull had said. He gave us each a long fly rod and a pair of cloth gloves, then led us along the river till we found room to fish.

"Now you kids pay attention," Mr. Bull said. "Any of you ever salmon fish before? . . . Didn't think so . . . Watch what I do . . . Throw it out, roll it easy . . ." *Plunk*. The lure, attached to a heavy lead weight, dropped into the fast current. "Let it sink to the bottom . . . Now, strip it!" He began yanking the line in with his left hand until the lure returned nearly to the tip of the pole. "Again, throw it, wait, then strip . . ."

Slowly, awkwardly, the three of us tried it. Mr. Bull set his rod down and helped us, first Sharon, then Erik K., then me. The gloves protected our

31

hands from the line, which could cut when we yanked it in. Mr. Bull spent a long time explaining patiently and correcting our technique.

Suddenly Sharon shouted. "I've got something! I've got one!"

Mr. Bull rushed to her. "That's it, hold tight. Reel in the slack—keep the tip of your rod up! Tighten down on your drag now . . . Work it back and forth . . . Give him a little line now . . . Let him run with it . . . Okay, now bring him in . . ."

He picked up a dip net and leaned out as Sharon slowly reeled the fish in. But before he could net it, the fish leaped out of the water, a beautiful, silvery creature, and then dove. Sharon fought to hold on.

"He's making a fight—that's all right, give him some line . . . Now work him back to you . . . Good, come on . . . Strong fellas, aren't they?"

We saw the salmon just under the water as Sharon pulled it near the bank. Mr. Bull scooped his blue net gently under the fish and lifted it out, thrashing.

"All right!" Erik and I shouted.

"Nice one!" Mr. Bull said, laying it gently on the grass. Erik and I set our rods down and went over to look.

The big fish had a dark back, silvery sides, and white belly. Its hooked jaws looked powerful.

"Wow, look at that!" Erik K. said.

"What do you think it weighs, Mr. Bull?" I asked.

"Ten pounds, easy."

But Sharon stared sadly at the gasping fish. "Do we have to kill it?" she asked. "Can't we let it go?"

Squatting beside the salmon, the bearded man gazed at her thoughtfully. "Well, now, that's a good question, Sharon ... Sure, we can let it go ... But you know this fish'll die in a few days anyway ... Life cycle of the salmon—they swim upstream to spawn and then they die ..."

"I don't care," she said. "I want to let this one go."

Mr. Bull nodded. "Well then, let's let it go." He quickly removed the hook from the creature's mouth. "Come on, Sharon, help me lift this old dip net ..." Together they carried the net back to the river and lowered it in.

At first, the salmon lay motionless in the cold water. But when the metal rim went below the surface, the fish thrashed desperately, slid over, and was gone. Sharon and Mr. Bull stared at the gray-green river.

"Well," Erik said, grabbing his rod, "I'm going to keep mine."

Mr. Bull nodded. "I've kept many, and I've let many go ... Know just how your sister feels ..." He patted Sharon's shoulder.

7

For several days we camped at the campground, fishing and taking short hikes into the
mountains. Slowly, we got used to steep trails and
chilly, sometimes rainy weather. On Sunday we
went to church in Soldotna, and it was funny to
hear gruff old Mr. Bull sing hymns along with the
rest of us.

Finally, Mr. Bull said we were ready to begin our
assignment. "Wasted enough time fishing," he muttered one morning over a breakfast of scrambled
eggs, fried salmon, and toast and jelly. "Time to get
to work . . . Kids must think you're on vacation or
something . . . You didn't come up here to play . . .
Earn your keep . . ."

We grinned at each other. We were used to Mr. Bull's grumblings by now.

We drove back to Anchorage, spent the night at the Bulls' house, then headed north the next morning toward Denali National Park.

"What should we do if we see a grizzly bear?" I asked, still half asleep, bouncing along in Mr. Bull's van.

"Fall down on your knees and pray," Mr. Bull retorted.

"Is it really that dangerous?" Sharon asked him.

"Dangerous? You crazy? Won't catch me up in those mountains . . ."

"Then why are you letting *us* go?" she asked.

He glanced at her. "Well, you're young . . . Run fast . . . Me, I'm too old . . . Ever tell you kids about the time a grizzly came after me?"

"No! Tell us!" we said.

"Me and Johnny Peters . . . Over around Wrangell . . . Camped out on the side of a mountain, nothin' but tundra, not a climbin' tree in sight . . . I saw a grizzly bear, an' I says, 'Johnny, a grizzly bear's comin'!' Crazy guy sat down on the ground, took his runnin' shoes out of his pack, and started puttin' 'em on. I says, 'What're you doing? You can't outrun a grizzly bear!' He just grinned, an' he says, 'I don't have to outrun the bear. I just have to outrun you!'"

Erik K. and Sharon burst out laughing. I just shook my head. "What's so funny?" I said. "I don't get it."

"It's a joke, dummy," Erik said. "The bear's going to stop when he catches the slow guy."

"Oh." I scowled. "That would probably be me, then."

"Ah, you kids don't have to worry," Mr. Bull said. "Too little for a bear to fool with . . . Wouldn't even make a mouthful . . . Now me, I'd make a whole meal . . ."

"What *do* we do if we see a bear, I mean really?" Sharon asked.

"Well, first off, don't eat in or near your tent . . . Eat at least a hundred yards away, got that? Important . . . And keep your food away from your tent . . . You were in the woods you could hang it from a tree, but you'll be above treeline . . . Make plenty of noise when you hike—don't want to surprise a bear, know what I mean? He might not like it . . . Here, got something for you. Erik K., reach in that box behind your seat . . . See those spray cans? Should be three of 'em . . ."

Erik K. pulled out three silver cans.

"Bear mace," Mr. Bull explained. "Got red pepper in it . . . Just point and shoot . . . Bears can't stand that stuff . . . Keep it in your pocket . . . If it doesn't work, well, maybe the bear likes his food spicy-hot . . ."

"Very funny," Sharon said.

"Hey, look at *that*," Erik said, pointing. Far ahead of us the dim outline of a mountain seemed to float in the sky.

36

"That's Denali, the big one," Mr. Bull said.

We stared in wonder at the high peak.

That afternoon we stopped for gas at a place called Bear Lodge. "This is where I'll stay," Mr. Bull said, motioning to the large, log-cabin style building with a long row of rooms beside it. "Eatin' steak in the restaurant and catchin' up on my reading while you kids're shiverin' in the rain . . . So you hike on up Bear Ridge, and just radio me when you see the crooks . . . I'll phone the rangers at Denali, and they'll send a chopper over, arrest the bad guys . . . Case closed . . . We all go home . . . Simple little job . . ."

"Too bad we can't think of a way to educate these people so they won't pick mushrooms to start with," Sharon said.

Erik snorted. "You're just saying that because that's what Miss Spice said."

"Thugs like these guys belong in jail," Mr. Bull grumbled.

"But how long can you keep them there?" Sharon said. "And when they get out, they'll go right back to smuggling mushrooms because that's the only way of life they know. But if we could teach them—"

"They go back to smuggling because they're nothing but crooks, Sharon," I said.

"But they're people, too," she said.

"Lowlifes," Mr. Bull said as we got out.

Erik filled the tank and Sharon cleaned the windshield while Mr. Bull and I went inside. A few customers sat at rustic tables in the small restaurant. Behind the counter stood a round-bellied man with a long white beard, his arms crossed and a scowl on his face.

Mr. Bull handed him a credit card. "Got any vacancies?"

"Yup."

"My name's Martin Bull. Like a room."

The man nodded as he rang up the gas.

"Be back in a little bit to get the key," Mr. Bull said. "Gotta run up the road a minute."

As we left, I said, "He wasn't very friendly, was he?"

Mr. Bull shook his head. "Probably been up in this north country too long . . . Got cabin fever . . ."

We piled into the van and Mr. Bull drove us a few miles up the road, turning in at a rustic wooden sign reading "Bear Ridge Trailhead." We stopped in a small, empty, gravel parking lot. We were surrounded by trees that gave the air an evergreen tang but blocked our view of the mountains.

"This is it," Mr. Bull said as we unloaded gear. "You kids got everything you need?"

"I think so," I said, hoisting my heavy pack and adjusting the brim of my baseball cap.

"What about a water filter . . . Got something to purify water?"

"Miss Spice packed us these," Erik said, holding up a small brown bottle.

"Iodine crystals, huh? Well, that should work . . . What about pocket knives?"

We stared at each other and shook our heads.

Mr. Bull grinned. "Didn't think so." He rummaged in the van and took out a paper sack, handing it to me. "One for each of you."

I pulled out a shiny red Swiss army knife. "Wow!" I said, handing the bag to Sharon.

"Neat!" she said, passing it to her brother. "What all does it have on it?"

"Two knife blades," I said, pulling the blades open, "a big one and a little one."

"Here's a screwdriver and a file on one blade," Erik said.

"A can opener and a bottle opener," I said.

"Scissors, saw blade—and an awl," Sharon said, ticking off the remaining blades.

Mr. Bull pulled a large, black, two-way radio from the van. "You remember how to use this, don't you?"

We nodded—he'd shown us the radio in Anchorage, making us repeat his instructions so we wouldn't forget. I grimaced as he stuffed the heavy radio into my pack.

"There's the trail," Mr. Bull said, pointing across the lot. "Just follow it . . . When you get to the top of the ridge, find somewhere you like and make camp

. . . Set up your telescope and go to work . . . I'll be down below at the lodge . . ."

Now that I was standing here, pack on my back, staring down a rugged trail into a dark forest, all of my fears about this trip came flooding back. "Mr. Bull, are you sure we'll be okay?"

"Okay? Sure you'll be okay . . . Three top fishermen like you kids . . . Got your bear mace, got your radio—call me if you need me—tents, food, sleeping bags . . . Be cozy as bugs in a rug . . . Go on now, get started!"

Sharon ran over and hugged him.

"You take care of these boys now, Sharon," Mr. Bull said. "They'll need you . . . Keep 'em out of trouble."

She nodded. We crossed the parking lot and entered the woods.

8

Erik led the way, followed by Sharon, with me last. The trail led through flat woods, full of smells of spruce and pine and minty-clean things like that. It curved through thick bushes higher than my head, and I could see how a bear could jump out and eat you before you knew it. Just to be on the safe side, I carried the can of mace in my hand.

The path took a sharp turn and angled uphill. It didn't take me long to figure out that I liked the trail a whole lot better when it was flat. Even though the weather was chilly and damp, I soon began to sweat. The bushes dripped from an earlier rain, so I was wet on the outside too. When I walked I felt hot and sweaty, but when I stopped to catch my breath a cold wind cut right through me.

"Hold up, you guys," I said, taking a breather.

Sharon stopped gladly, but Erik K. looked impatient. He was used to exercising all the time, and it seemed like he never got tired.

"We've got a long way to go," he said after a few minutes.

I nodded and we started walking again.

"What are all these things?" I called to Sharon, kicking at some brown blobs in the path.

She paused to look. "Bear scat."

"Scat?"

"Droppings."

Uh-oh. Where there were droppings there had to be droppers. I shifted my can of mace into my shooting hand.

"Hey, look at all these berries!" Erik said. He pointed to red and yellow clusters dangling from trailside bushes.

"These are the wild raspberries Mr. Bull was telling us about," Sharon said, popping one into her mouth.

Erik tried one. "Yum!" He grabbed more.

I nibbled at one—sweet and juicy. "So this is what the bears eat," I said, tossing a couple more in my mouth. "I always wondered how a big old bear could find enough food to live on. Now I know."

For a while we stuffed ourselves in silence, handful after handful.

"Just think how good they'd be on frozen yogurt," Erik K. said.

"Or in cobbler," I added.

We ate some more, then Sharon said, "We'd better move on, guys. If we keep eating we will get a stomachache."

Reluctantly, we left the berry patch behind and continued walking. But there were lots more berry bushes along the trail as we hiked, and now and then a berry looked so big and juicy I just had to pick it. Then the raspberry bushes started to get further and further apart, and pretty soon there weren't any at all. I stopped looking for berries then and started looking around. There were fewer trees, too, and they were smaller than before, almost stunted-looking. As we huffed and puffed steadily uphill, the trees became so small they looked like scrubby bushes, and then they disappeared altogether. Gray, mossy-looking stuff covered the ground.

"Tundra," Erik said.

"I guess we're above the treeline now," Sharon said.

Now that there were no trees, we had a clear view of Bear Ridge looming high above us. The trail zigzagged up its side like a pencil mark.

"Looks like a long way to the top," I said, buttoning my jacket against the wind.

We trudged for awhile, up and up. Then we paused for another rest. Not even Erik was used to this kind of exercise.

"Just think if we hadn't done all that hiking on bleachers," Sharon said, panting.

I leaned over, my hands on my knees. "We'd never make it." Then I noticed a bunch of little round things in the tundra. "Hey, blueberries!"

"Yeah. Didn't Mr. Bull say something about low-bush blueberries?" Erik said, kneeling to try them. "Wow, these are great!"

We took off our packs and dropped to our hands and knees to feast again.

"They're everywhere!" I said. "There must be a million."

"More than that," Sharon said. "They're all over the tundra, and the tundra goes on forever."

"No wonder bears are so fat," her brother said.

Pausing, I glanced up. "Uh-oh," I said in a low voice. "Speaking of bears—take a look!"

9

The bears were a long way off, across a steep valley on a hillside opposite us, three small black shapes moving slowly up the slope.

"Looks like a mama and two cubs," Sharon said.

"Grizzlies or black bears?" Erik wondered.

"Grizzlies are brown and black bears are black," Sharon said. "Those look black to me."

"You can't always tell by the color," I said, pleased to know something Sharon didn't about wildlife. "I looked it up before we left. The book says sometimes grizzlies are black and sometimes black bears are brown."

"Then how do you tell the difference?" Erik asked.

"You can't always. But usually a grizzly *is* brown and a black *is* black. Plus, grizzlies tend to be bigger than blacks."

"I'd just as soon stay away from both of them," Erik said.

We watched the bears, which seemed in no hurry to climb their mountain.

"I'll bet they're eating berries," Sharon said.

"Yeah. That's why they're taking their time," Erik agreed. "How far off do you think they are?"

"Close to a mile?" I guessed.

"I hope they can't smell us from there," Sharon said. "Bears have really good noses, I do know that."

"Wait a minute. I know how we can tell," Erik said. He stuck his finger in his mouth, then held it up. "Nope. The wind is blowing from them to us, so they probably can't smell us."

His sister looked at him as if he were crazy. "How do you know?"

He grinned. "I saw it on TV. You wet your finger and hold it up, and whichever side gets cold first is the side the wind is blowing from."

"Cool!" I said, trying it. Sharon did too.

"Well, I'm just glad those bears are over there and not over here," I said.

We put our packs on and continued hiking, but a little more cautiously now that we'd actually seen bears. If there were bears eating berries over there,

there could be bears eating berries over here. Fortunately, up here above treeline we could see for miles. Tundra-covered mountains stretched in all directions. Below us lay dark green forest.

"Hey, look at Denali now," Sharon said in a hushed voice.

We turned and looked behind us. Off in the distance, a huge range of snowy peaks floated in the air like castles, with clouds trailing around them. One peak stood higher than all the others.

"Bet we can really see it good when we get to the top of Bear Ridge," Erik K. said.

Suddenly we heard a whistle.

"Who was that?" I said, scanning the slope.

We peered all around but saw no one. Then Sharon pointed and giggled. A furry little creature, not much bigger than a squirrel, watched us from a knoll.

"A prairie dog!" Erik said.

"That's a marmot," Sharon said. "They're nearly the same." She grinned. "I did some reading about Alaskan wildlife, too."

"Okay, if you're so smart, what are those?" Erik asked her.

Just a few yards up the path, a group of funny-looking birds walked along with their heads bobbing up and down.

"Some kind of quail," she whispered. "Wait a minute, it'll come to me. I know—they're ptarmigan!"

"Why aren't they afraid of us?" I said, surprised the birds didn't fly away.

"Let me see how close I can get," Sharon said quietly, and inched toward the fat creatures. They craned their necks to stare at her, and scurried a few steps away. Sharon continued to creep toward them, making a "chukka-chukka-chukka" sound. The ptarmigan lowered their heads into their bunched-up chests and watched her curiously.

When she was just a few feet away, Sharon squatted and held her hand out. One of the ptarmigan stared at her with cocked head, then took a few sideways steps in her direction.

"Look!" Erik whispered. "It's coming right up to her."

The bird was so close Sharon could have grabbed it. But she just waited. With a few more steps the ptarmigan stopped next to her hand, and Sharon rubbed its neck gently. The bird closed its eyes and extended its neck to be scratched.

"I knew she had a way with animals, but wow!" I said.

The other birds pecked at the ground, and finally their brave friend joined them. Sharon walked back to us, grinning. "Aren't they neat?"

Suddenly the birds flew up like a feathery explosion. Flying low to the ground, they scattered across the mountainside and disappeared just as a shadow floated across the tundra right where they'd been.

Erik looked up. "Is that what I think it is?"

"An eagle!" Sharon said.

10

The huge bird, its wings outspread, coasted through the air, peering at the ground.

"No wonder the ptarmigan flew off," I said.

"That's a bald eagle," Erik said. "See the white head?"

The giant bird circled a few times, then flew off over the mountains.

"Did you see how wide his wings were?" I said. "I'll bet they were wider than we are tall."

"They can get up to six or eight feet across," Sharon said, nodding.

A gust of cold wind whisked across the tundra. A few moments later rain began to fall, and we quick-ly pulled out our ponchos. They were extra long, fitting over our packs, and we each wore a different color.

Erik K. chuckled. "You two look like some kind of giant goony birds," he said.

I glanced down at my bright blue poncho and over at Sharon's purple one. Erik K. wore bright yellow.

"You look just as goofy," Sharon giggled at her brother. "Like a big yellow chicken."

"I don't know which is worse, a goony bird or a chicken," he said with a grin. "Well, let's get going."

We walked quickly in the cold rain. I couldn't wait to pitch a tent and cook a hot meal. And to think this was summer!

We hiked for hours. The rain finally ended. When we neared the top of the ridge, Erik paused. "At least the rain has stopped," he said, peering at the gray sky.

"Yeah," Sharon said. Then she gasped. "Look!"

Glancing back the way we had come, we saw Denali, its snowy slopes golden in the evening sunlight. The clouds around it were breaking up, showing patches of blue sky. The lower mountains around Denali also glowed silver and gold, decorated with snow like giant cakes.

"I think we should make camp here," Erik said, looking all around us. "There'll probably be less wind than on top of the ridge."

"There's a stream right down there," I said.

"And here's a flat spot for a tent," Sharon added.

"Too bad we can't have a campfire," I said, rubbing my arms.

"If there *was* any wood it would be soaking wet," Erik K. said.

We dropped our packs gratefully and rested a few minutes. Then we teamed up to pitch the two small dome tents side by side.

"Sure is pretty up here," I said, straightening up after pushing the last tent stake in, gazing at the miles and miles of mountains and at massive Denali across the big valley from us. "What's that river?"

Sharon pulled a map from her pack and unfolded it. "That's the Chulitna River. That mountain to the right of Denali is Mount Silverthrone. It's only 13,220 feet."

Erik laughed. "*Only* 13,220 feet!"

She grinned. "Well, that's small compared to Denali. Okay, the big one on the left is Mount Hunter, 14,573 feet."

"Are those glaciers?" I said, pointing to large fields of snow lying between the mountains.

She nodded. "The big one on the left is Ruth Glacier."

"How high are we, does it say?" Erik asked.

"Well, the top of Bear Ridge is 4,558 feet."

Erik nodded. "And we're probably a couple hundred feet below it."

"Man, if it's this cold here, think how it must be on Denali!" I said.

"Yeah, let's fix something hot," Erik said. "Sharon, why don't you set up the telescope while Eric C. and I cook supper."

"Okay," she said. "Remember to take the food away from the tents."

"How about over there?" he said, pointing to some rocks several hundred feet away.

"I'll fill the pot with water and meet you over there," I said. I climbed down to the stream, fetched the water, and joined Erik at the rocks. He was opening packages of dehydrated beef and noodles.

"Did you purify it?" he asked me as he fired up the stove.

"Don't need to if we're going to cook it," I said. "That's just for drinking water."

He nodded, setting the pot over the flame. We snacked on cheese and crackers. From the rocks where we sat, about a football field's distance away from camp, the two dome tents looked like bright little toys and Sharon like a little munchkin or something as she crouched to look through the telescope. Then she turned toward us, cupped her hands, and yelled something we couldn't make out. She motioned with her arm for us to come back.

We jogged over. "Take a look," she said. "It's neat!" I knelt and peered through the lens. The slopes of Mount Denali, which had seemed so far away, suddenly appeared close. I could make out craggy rocks, blue snowy crevices, and streaks of golden glacier.

"Wow!" I breathed.

"Let me see," said Erik.

"We need to aim it farther down to find smugglers," Sharon said. "Mr. Bull said they're getting mushrooms from the lower slopes."

When her brother finished looking, she tilted it gradually lower. "This looks like a good spot, right near the bottom," she said. She glanced at her map. "I think that's the Moose's Tooth."

I chuckled, not sure whether she was serious. "The what?"

"One of those lower mountains. See here on the map? About 10,000 feet. There's Buckskin Glacier."

"Let me look," Erik said, and Sharon moved aside. "I see it. There's the Moose's Tooth, and Buckskin Glacier, and—hey! That looks like people! Look, Sharon!"

She quickly pressed an eye against the rim of the lens. "Where?"

"Lower right."

"Sure enough! I see a red jacket and a blue jacket."

"Let me see, let me see," I said. Peering through the glass, I saw two people walking slowly across the slope. Now and then one bent over and picked up something from the ground.

Smugglers!

11

I looked up from the telescope. "We hit the jackpot, guys!"

"How do we know they're the smugglers?" Erik asked.

"Watch and you'll see."

"Yeah," Sharon said, gazing through the scope. "They're picking things off the ground and putting them into bags. That's got to be them!"

"Are we super agents, or what?" I said. "Talk about fast work. I'll just radio Mr. Bull and he can call the rangers." I pulled the radio from my pack. "They'll fly in and arrest the guys, and we can go home tomorrow!"

"Go home already? Do we have to?" Sharon asked.

"We just got here," said Erik. "I wanted to do some more hiking."

"Yeah, but it's so *cold*," I said. "Besides, it's not like we just got to Alaska. We've seen a lot of it already, with Mr. Bull."

Sharon sighed.

"Hey, do you think we have time to hike back down today, before it gets dark?" I asked.

Erik looked at the sky doubtfully. "Better radio Mr. Bull first. He'll tell us what to do."

I unsnapped the leather cover and turned the radio on. "This is Sockeye Charlie calling Mad Bull," I said, using code words Mr. Bull had taught us. "Come in, Mad Bull."

The radio crackled. "This is Mad Bull. Over."

"Mad Bull, the collectors have been spotted," I said. "You've got a green light. Repeat, a green light. Over."

More static. "We've got an emergency here, Sockeye Charlie. Return to base immediately. Repeat, return to base immediately. Out."

"Wait! Emergency? What kind of emergency? Over." There was no answer. "Come in, Mad Bull. What kind of emergency? Do you mean return tonight, or what? Over."

No answer.

"Come in, Mad Bull. Come in, Mad Bull. Aw, come on, Mr. Bull, answer me."

Silence and static. I stared at my friends. "What do you think he meant?"

"Man, I don't know," Erik K. said, looking surprised and worried.

"Do you think he meant tonight?"

"He couldn't mean that," Sharon said. "It's too late."

Erik looked at his watch. "Wow—it's 8 o'clock."

"That northern sun fools us," Sharon said.

We sat quietly for a few seconds, thinking. Suddenly Erik's eyes opened wide. "Oh no, the noodles!" He jumped up and dashed toward the rocks where we'd started supper cooking.

"Come on, let's eat," Sharon said, brushing herself off and following him. "A hot meal will do us good."

We sat on cold rocks eating a gloomy supper. As if to match our mood, gray clouds moved in again, hiding Denali.

"Well," I said, "do you think he meant for all of us to go back, or just me?"

"Why would he mean just you?" Sharon asked.

"I don't know, but he said, 'Sockeye Charlie, return to base,' remember? And I'm Sockeye Charlie."

"I guess he might have wanted someone to stay up here with the scope to guide the rangers over the radio," Erik K. said doubtfully.

"Look," I said, "here's an idea. First thing in the morning I'll hike back down. When I get to the highway I'll walk or hitchhike back to the lodge. You two can stay here, and I'll radio you as soon as I get there and let you know what to do."

"Why don't I go instead?" Erik K. offered. "I can probably make it faster."

"And me stay here with Sharon?"

He nodded. "Why not?"

"What if a bear attacks the camp?" I asked. "She'll be better off with you here than me."

"You're being silly," Sharon said. But she sounded a little nervous.

"You guys have mace," Erik said. "What do you expect me to do with a bear—kick it?"

"It might be better if you stayed though, Erik K.," Sharon said.

"I'll bet I can make it in a few hours," I said. "It's all downhill."

"I wonder what the emergency is," Sharon mused.

"Who knows?" I said. "We'll find out tomorrow. Probably nothing serious."

Erik frowned. "I don't know. I don't like any of this. Why would he tell us there's an emergency if it wasn't something serious? He didn't even sound excited about the green light." He scratched a mosquito bite on his neck thoughtfully. "Still, if we all go down, we'll lose track of the smugglers."

"I think Eric C. should go," Sharon said softly. "He can find out what's wrong and radio us."

Erik K. stared moodily at the distant mountain range. At last he nodded, obviously unhappy with the plan.

12

We crawled into our tents at 10 o'clock, but I had trouble falling asleep because it wasn't dark at all. Finally I lay a shirt across my eyes to block the light, and dozed off.

When I woke, I thought I had slept late because it was bright outside, but it was just 6 a.m. I snoozed a little longer, then dressed and went out.

The world was covered in mist. Denali was invisible, and even the nearby top of Bear Ridge was hidden. Everything seemed gray and muffled. Not far below, I could hear the chuckling sound the little stream made. A marmot whistled somewhere. Hunching my shoulders against the chill, I made my way down to the stream to wash my face and collect a pot of water.

When I got back, Erik and Sharon were up. "Nobody got attacked by bears in the night, huh?" I joked.

They grinned sleepily.

We made hot oatmeal for breakfast, topped with wild blueberries, and ate on the rocks away from the tent.

"We're not going to spy on any smugglers in this," Erik complained, waving his arm at the heavy fog.

"Maybe it'll burn off soon," Sharon said.

I finished eating and stood up. "Well, I'm going to pack up and hit the trail."

"Sure you don't want us to come with you?" Sharon asked.

"No," Erik answered for me. "I got to thinking last night. If Mr. Bull *doesn't* want us all to come back down the mountain yet, then we'll just have to lug all this gear back up here after we see him. Better to find out for sure." He rubbed his arms in the chilly air.

After brushing my teeth, I loaded my pack quickly and checked my wrist compass. "Well, I'll radio you as soon as I get down." I said.

"Be careful."

"I will." I waved and set off down the trail. Relieved to be moving at last and glad the trail was downhill, I sped along, filling my lungs with brisk air, sniffing all the clean tundra smells. Little flowers nestled in the lichen. Even though the tundra appeared gray at first glance, up close it was full of colors.

Though the fog was thick, I could easily follow the trail. But there were no mountain views today. I remembered Mr. Bull's warning about surprising a bear on the trail, so I decided to sing.

I thought I remembered a character in *Tom Sawyer* who walked along singing "Buffalo Gals" and pretending to blow a steamboat whistle. I cleared my throat.

> *"Buffalo gals won't you come out tonight,*
> *"Come out tonight, come out tonight?*
> *"Buffalo gals won't you come out tonight,*
> *"And dance by the light of the moon?*
> *"WOOOO! WOOOO!"*

A covey of ptarmigan exploded from some bushes.

"Hey, you guys, I didn't know my singing was that bad," I told them.

My voice also woke up some marmots, who popped out of their holes and began to whistle.

"Not bad," I said to them. "See if you can follow this tune." I whistled "Buffalo Gals." But the marmots couldn't get the hang of it. They just made one or two high notes and stared at me.

"Hey, I may be crazy, but I'll bet every bear in ten miles hears me!" I hollered, and laughed.

But the sound of my voice died away quickly, swallowed up by fog, and I shivered. Despite the animals and birds, this was a lonely place.

At last the trail entered the forest. Trees dripped water all around. It was dark and cold and eerie in here. But there were also heaps of raspberry bushes, and I stopped to snack. The juicy fruit cheered me up. "Delicious!" I said aloud, just in case any bears were dining nearby.

I started again, walking faster in the gloomy forest, anxious to get back to the lodge. The path twisted and turned. I kept expecting to come to the parking lot, but I seemed to be taking forever to get there. At last I stopped to catch my breath.

There was a sudden, low sound—a growl? Every muscle tensed—and then I realized it was a motor starting. The parking lot! I ran out into the open just in time to see a silver jeep pulling away.

"Wait!" I shouted, waving my arms as I ran. "Wait!"

To my relief the brake lights lit up and the jeep stopped. As I trotted toward it, a man leaned out the driver's door. I recognized the long white beard of the lodge owner.

"Hey, kid," he said. "I been waiting on you."

"But where's Mr. Bull?"

He shook his head grimly. "Emergency. Had to fly back to Anchorage. Get in."

13

"What happened?" I asked as we drove away from the trail and turned onto the highway.

"Very sad," the man said. Despite his size he spoke in a high-pitched, almost squeaky voice. "Mrs. Bull fell and broke both her legs. Mr. Bull went up to the park and caught a plane back to Anchorage."

"Wow! How did she break both legs?"

"She was on a fishing boat and she fell when some waves hit."

"Fishing boat? But what about work? She's a nurse—"

"Yeah, well, she took the day off." He changed the subject. "Bet you got lonely up on that mountain, didn't you, kid?"

Lonely? Of course not! Didn't he remember Erik and—then I remembered: they'd stayed out with the van when Mr. Bull and I had gone in to get his room. So this old guy thought I was the only one. Good—because something fishy was definitely going on. Just then we drove past Bear Lodge without stopping.

"Hey! Where are we going?" I said.

"I'm taking you to Anchorage to see Mr. Bull."

"No, you're not! What's going on?" Something was wrong, very wrong. Frightened, I grabbed the door handle and looked out the window. Were we going too fast for me to jump out?

"Don't be stupid, kid," he said.

I looked back around. The bearded man was holding a pistol. Automatically, I grabbed for my mace. But he shook his head, waved his pistol at me, and told me to throw it into the back. "Just calm down and everything will be okay," he said. Then he chuckled. "You and Mr. Bull thought you'd pull a fast one, didn't you?"

"What do you mean?"

"Don't play innocent with me, sonny boy. You're trying to catch mushroom collectors. He put you up on the mountain to watch and he stayed down here with a radio."

Still no mention of Erik K. and Sharon, so they were safe. "How'd you find out?" I asked.

He snickered. "I run a tight ship at Bear Lodge. I got the rooms bugged and the phones tapped, just in case federal agents like Bull come snooping around. Bull phoned his wife to tell her he was all

right, and he told her Sockeye Charlie—that's you—was up on the mountain and he was waiting to hear from you. You think I'm dumb? It was easy to figure out you guys' plan."

"So you tricked him into flying back to Anchorage."

"Soon as he heard his old lady broke her legs, he told me to arrange for him to catch a plane. I asked him about the kid I'd seen him with, namely you. He was so upset about his wife he gave me the radio and asked me to call you and tell you he'd be back soon and to hang tight. Even told me your code name, the dummy! Then he took off like a singed rabbit to catch that plane." He chuckled. "The guy must really think a lot of his old lady, huh?"

"That was you on the radio, then. But you didn't tell me to hang tight. You told me to come down. What are you going to do with me now?" I wiped my sweaty palms on my jeans.

"Couldn't leave you up on the mountain watching my collectors, now could I? You're the only witness. All I can say is, the federal government must be in bad shape, hiring a kid as a spy."

He turned off the highway onto on a small dirt road. We bounced along the rutted road for a few miles without saying anything, and then he stopped beside a parked maroon pickup sitting high on mud-caked tires. Behind the steering wheel a skinny blond man with a mustache sat sleeping. He wore thick glasses, a Florida Marlins baseball cap, and a faded jean jacket. His head lay back and a fly circled his open mouth.

The bearded man honked his horn. The man in the maroon pickup jumped, accidentally swallowing the fly, which turned his face red and made him cough violently.

My driver laughed, his belly shaking against the steering wheel. "That'll teach you to sleep on the job, Jamie."

"You didn't have to scare me like that, Paul!" Jamie said.

"Here's our visitor. Kid, you go with him."

As I stepped out of the jeep, I thought about making a run for it. Then I remembered Paul's gun.

"Hop wight in here," said Jamie, who seemed to have trouble pronouncing his r's. At least he sounded friendly. "What's your name, anyway?"

"Eric. Eric Sterling." I climbed onto the high seat as he cranked the motor in a cloud of blue smoke.

"See you later, Paul," he shouted over the growl of the engine.

Paul nodded. "Don't waste any time, now. That agent'll probably be back tomorrow. And he'll be a mite peeved."

"Wight!" Jamie pulled the pickup onto the narrow dirt road that led deep into the forest.

Only then did I realize that I'd left my pack, and my bear mace, in the jeep.

14

"Where are you taking me?" I asked.

"Our camp. I guess you know, we're mushwoom collectors." He said it almost proudly.

"I guess *you* know that's against the law?"

"You mean that stupid park wegulation? Nobody pays any attention to that. I mean, what's the diffewence between picking mushwooms inside the park or outside the park?"

"I don't know, but if all the mushrooms disappear the forests will die, and so will the wildlife."

He laughed, like I was joking. He had a funny, snickery laugh that blew the wiry strands of his reddish-blond mustache.

"Seriously!" I insisted. "Mushrooms bring up nutrients so other plants can feed on them."

He chortled louder, pounding the steering wheel. "Hey, they're just mushwooms, you know? Gimme a bweak!"

"Well, if they're just mushrooms, why do people pay so much for them?"

"'Cause they're good to eat, man. At least, that's what they say." He turned onto another dirt road, even narrower and bumpier than the one we'd been on—really just two tire tracks through the forest, with grass and bushes between. "Hang on, Ewic, it gets bumpy from here."

The truck bounced roughly on the rocky, rutted lane. We splashed through several mud puddles, then came to a wide, pebbly stream.

"Here we go!" Jamie said.

We bumped painfully across the creek—my head almost hit the pickup's ceiling once—and into the woods on the other side. Several creeks and a few bruises later, we arrived in a clearing where a saggy green tent stood.

"We've been camped here a week, picking," Jamie said. "But we've got them just about picked out awound here." He cut the motor and we climbed out. Jamie yawned and stretched with a happy groan. "My fwiends are out collecting. They'll be back soon, for lunch."

"How many friends?" I asked, looking around.

Jamie slapped a mosquito. "Two. Will and Donnie. Boy, these mosquitoes are tough!" He sprayed himself with repellent and passed me the can. "We were camped up on the mountain, but Paul made us come down here where we wouldn't be as visible. Like Vienna sausages?"

"Sure."

"We keep our food way over there, in case of bears. Come on." He pulled a shotgun from the truck rack and led the way across the clearing to a huge ice chest sealed with a padlock.

"What's the gun for?" I said with a nervous chuckle. "I'm not dangerous."

"Bears! Gwizzly! I don't go anywhere without this." He patted the gun. "Short-bawweled twelve-gauge, loaded with slugs." He leaned it against a tree and opened the ice chest.

Just then someone shouted: "Hey, Jamie! Lunch ready?"

I looked across the clearing. A tall, skinny man walked toward us, followed by a much shorter one. Both carried big cloth bags that looked mostly empty.

"Hey, you guys," Jamie said as they came up. "This is Ewic. Ewic, meet Donnie and Will."

"Pleased to meet you," said Donnie, who must have been seven feet tall but was thin as a stork, with a scruffy dark beard. He wore khaki pants, a blue nylon parka, tennis shoes and a floppy hat.

Will wore a red rainsuit even though it wasn't raining. He had sandy brown hair, glasses, and a shy face. "Hi, Eric," he said.

All three of these guys seemed friendly. I didn't really feel like a prisoner.

For lunch we had canned Vienna sausages, crackers, and water, then Jamie hauled out a sack of chocolate chip cookies for dessert.

"Mushrooms getting scarce," Donnie said with a burp. "'Bout time to break camp and move on. Paul say where he wants to send us this time?"

"He seemed pwetty nervous, 'specially after catching these spies," Jamie said.

Donnie stared at me, but he looked more sad than threatening. "What you spying on us for anyway, kid? Why don't you mind your own business?"

I tried to explain the importance of mushrooms, but they just snorted or laughed.

"I think we oughta get out of Denali," Will said. "Maybe go down to the Chugach Mountains." He pulled a box of floss from a pocket and began cleaning his teeth energetically.

"Too close to Anchorage. Probably a lot of collectors," Donnie said. "Plus, we got this kid to deal with."

"Yeah," Jamie said, adding quickly, "no offense, Ewic." Then he mumbled, "I don't see why Paul had to go and nab him."

"Shut up!" Will said. "Nobody nabbed anybody. Eric's just visiting, right, Eric?"

"Well, not really."

"We'll take Eric home anytime he gets ready," Will said, rising.

"Okay, I'm ready," I said.

"Yep, anytime he's ready."

"Hey, I said I'm ready!"

Will yawned and stretched. "Think I'll take a nap."

15

That afternoon I stayed in camp with Jamie while Will and Donnie went collecting again, grumbling about having to do all the work while Jamie was babysitting. Jamie and I sat leaning against boulders, staring at the treetops and the cloudy sky.

"How'd you guys get started picking mushrooms?" I asked.

He swatted at a bug. "We used to wun a sporting goods store in Flowida, and we'd come to Alaska evewy summer on vacation. Finally we decided we liked it so much here that we'd move. So we opened a store in Anchowage, but unfortunately it isn't doing so hot."

"Why not?"

"Well, our main line was surfboards and snorkels and stuff. We thought we'd corner the market here, but it seems like nobody's intewested in our pwoducts."

I tried not to laugh. Surfboards and snorkels in Alaska?

"So one day we met Paul, and he told us we could make some money helping him collect mushwooms," Jamie continued. "He loaned us some money up fwont to help keep our sporting goods store open while we picked. But we can't seem to pick enough to get that loan all paid off, so we just keep picking and picking."

"You mean you're not even making any money from the mushrooms?"

"Oh, he gives us some. But mostly he just knocks it off our debt."

I shook my head. "Sounds like you got taken, Jamie. I think this guy Paul has you right where he wants you."

"Not weally. We'd have pwobably lost our business by now if it wasn't for Paul. He's a nice guy, basically."

"If he's so nice, why did he kidnap me?"

"Oh, come on, Ewic, he didn't kidnap you. He told us that other guy, Mr. Bull, had to get home on an emergency, and it wouldn't be safe for you to be out here all alone. That's all."

"Oh yeah? Then why did he pull a pistol on me?"

Jamie's eyebrows went up. "Pistol?"

"That's right."

He thought for a minute, then shrugged. "Pwobably a joke—a toy gun or something. What do you think we are, cwiminals? Gee whiz."

"Okay, if you're not criminals, take me back to Anchorage."

"We will, but wight now we're busy, you know? I mean, hey, you can walk out if you want, but it must be twenty miles back to the main woad, and even then you're in the middle of nowhere. Just quit wowwying, we'll take care of you." He patted his gun. "Yes sir, if a bear attacks, I'm weady!"

Late that afternoon Will and Donnie returned, their sacks still mostly empty. We ate Vienna sausages and beans for supper. Afterward Donnie said, "Well, I'm ready to turn in. Where's the kid going to sleep?"

"In the tent with us, I guess," Jamie said.

"You mean in the green monster?" Will said with a sneer, glancing at the sagging green tent as he flossed his teeth vigorously.

"Hey, how was I supposed to know it was going to leak?" Jamie protested.

"It's your tent. You could have tested it first," Donnie said.

Jamie peeked at the sky. "Maybe it won't wain tonight."

I shook my head. Sporting-goods-store owners who can't pick a tent that doesn't leak. "I could sleep in the truck," I said.

"Yeah, that's a good idea. Put him in the truck," Donnie said. "Just be sure to keep the key."

"Doesn't matter. I don't know how to drive," I told them.

"Hey, Ewic, if you see a bear tonight, honk that horn," Jamie said.

"Bear!" Donnie said, rising. "That Jamie's got bears on the brain."

"Hey, there are lots of bears awound here," Jamie retorted.

"Yeah, right. And how many have we seen so far?"

"That doesn't mean we won't see some."

"I saw three bears yesterday," I said.

"Where?" they all asked at once.

"Over near Bear Ridge."

They relaxed. "That's a long way from here," Jamie said.

"We don't have an extra sleeping bag, but we do have a lot of coats you can wrap up in," Will said as we crossed the clearing.

"I had one, but I left my pack in the jeep," I complained.

Donnie was so tall he almost had to bend over to pat my shoulder. "Don't worry, kid—we'll take care of you."

In the truck I slept comfortably, bundled in soft coats and sweaters. If a bear came, I never knew about it.

Next morning we were having breakfast—Vienna sausages and pop-tarts—when Paul drove up in his silver jeep. As he walked over to us, his long white beard bouncing against his round belly, he looked like a sinister Santa Claus.

"Boys, I think it's about time you pulled up stakes," he squeaked.

Donnie nodded. "Yeah, they're about all picked out around here."

"There's an old trapper's cabin on the south side of the park," Paul said. "Should be good pickin' around there."

Jamie frowned. "I'm wowwied about these wegulations Ewic keeps talking about."

"I was thinking," Donnie said. "Maybe we should go down to the Chugach. Wouldn't have to worry about the law."

"Don't you guys get it?" Paul asked, disgusted. "*Everybody* picks in places like the Chugach because it's not against the law there—at least not yet. That's why those places are picked out. People are too chicken to pick mushrooms in a national park because they're afraid of the rules. Well, good—that means more mushrooms for us."

"But what's the penalty if we get caught?" Will asked.

"No big deal—probably just a fine. But think of all the money we'll be making. We can afford the fine. And don't forget, you owe me."

"How could we ever forget?" Donnie said with a sigh.

Jamie slapped his neck. "Well, I'm weady to get out of this place anyway. Too many mosquitoes."

16

Jamie and I rode in the back of the maroon pick-up down the bumpy dirt road through the forest and out onto the main highway. A plane buzzed overhead and I wondered if Mr. Bull was on it. What would he do when he got back to Bear Lodge? Would he, Erik K. and Sharon ever find me? I wasn't too worried about Jamie, Donnie, and Will, but that Paul bothered me. When he said itch, they scratched.

"When are you guys going to let me go home?" I asked Jamie.

"Pwobably as soon as we finish at this next place—in a few days," he shouted over the rush of chilly wind.

I was going to ask him more but the truck turned off onto a rough gravel road and I had to grab something to keep from bouncing out. Many miles of twisty, steep, narrow road brought us to a run-down old shack at the edge of a lake where the forest ended. On the other side lay open tundra.

"Hey, this is neat," said Jamie, climbing out and dusting off his pants. "We can do some twout fishing, Ewic."

"What makes you think you'll have time to fish?" Donnie asked. "You're gonna be collecting mushrooms with Will and me."

"I thought you wanted me to watch Ewic."

"No, Will and I had a better idea. Eric here can help us pick. That way he can't turn us in, 'cause he'll be breaking the law too."

"No way," I said. "I'm not picking any mushrooms."

"We got that figured out too." Will grinned. "No mushrooms, no food."

Donnie laughed and patted my belly. "Looks like you need to lose a few pounds anyway."

"No fair!" I said.

"Oh, come on, Ewic, it's only mushwooms," Jamie said.

"Anyway, let's get this gear loaded into the cabin and get to work," Donnie said.

We carried sleeping bags and food into the dark, musty shack.

"Whose cabin is this?" I asked. It looked like it hadn't been used for years.

"Belongs to the Park Service now," Donnie said. "It was probably built a hundred years ago."

"Wow." I ran my fingers over the rough-hewn logs. The small building had one room, no windows, a dirt floor, and a crude stone fireplace. "Must have been lonely living here."

"Some old trapper built this, I'd guess," Donnie said.

Outside, Donnie and Will pulled four empty bags from the back of the truck. They handed me one, and I took it reluctantly.

"Remember," Donnie said, "no mushrooms, no food. Jamie, you and Eric go around that side of the lake. Will and I'll take this side."

"Let's go, Ewic," Jamie said.

"Whichever team picks the least mushrooms has to cook supper," Will said.

"Hey, that's not fair!" Jamie said, but Will and Donnie just laughed as they strolled away.

Jamie and I walked through the woods along the lakeshore.

"Don't you ever get tired of carrying that gun?" I asked. His shotgun hung from a sling around his shoulder.

He shook his head. "No way. What would *you* do if a bear charged wight now?"

"Run," I said.

"Bears can wun thirty miles an hour."

"Wow. Uh, climb a tree?"

"Bears can climb twees, even gwizzlies."

"Play dead."

"Some bears will just eat you if you play dead."

"Pray then, I guess."

"That's wight. Pway old Jamie won't miss. Hey, here's one." Bending down, he picked a mushroom and held it up. "This is the kind we're looking for."

"Jamie, I'm not picking any mushrooms."

"It's just a way to make sure you don't turn us in."

"I can't promise that either."

"Aw, come on, man. We been nice to you. What kind of fwiend are you, anyway?"

I shrugged, embarrassed and uneasy. They *had* been nice to me, it was true. I didn't feel good about turning them in. But they were breaking the law. And I was working for WSI.

"Here, I'll put this in your sack and say you picked it," he said, reaching for my bag.

"No!" I jerked away. "I'm just not going to do it."

"Yeah, well, I'll bet you will when you get hungwy." He tossed the mushroom into his sack.

A brisk wind blew across the lake. Jamie stooped over frequently, gathering. At the edge of the forest I spotted a big raspberry thicket and began popping berries into my mouth.

"Hey, no mushrooms, no food!" Jamie said.

"You can't stop me from picking berries," I said. "This is public land."

Jamie thought about it a minute, then shrugged. "I guess you're wight." He set down his gun and his bag and joined me.

I wasn't all that hungry, but since I probably wouldn't get any more food in camp, I ate all I could hold. Then I had an even better idea—the sack! I quickly began shoving handfuls of berries into it.

"You sure make a lot of noise when you eat, Ewic," Jamie said. "You sound like a pig."

I froze, suddenly ice cold. "I thought that was you. I'm not eating."

We both looked up at the same instant. Just a few yards away the bushes were moving as something big and noisy moved through them.

Jamie and I shouted at once. "Bear!"

17

I made a run for it but tripped over a log and fell flat on my face. Jamie was right behind me, and he jumped over me and began climbing a tree. Since it had no lower limbs he shinnied up it like a possum with its tail on fire.

I jumped up and hit the ground sprinting, trying to get as far away as fast as possible. I took a terrified look over my shoulder to see how much time I had before the bear ate me for lunch—and stopped. "Look, Jamie!" I said, pointing.

A black bear was scooting across the tundra, trying to get away from us as fast as we were trying to get away from it.

Jamie slid slowly down the tree, his clothes speckled with bark and sap.

"What happened to your gun?" I asked, still panting.

"Uh—I guess it's still lying over there by the berries."

I laughed, shaking with relief. Sheepishly, he joined in.

"Good thing that bear didn't want any meat, because he sure could have had us," I said as we crept back to the berry thicket.

"Don't know why I didn't think about my gun," Jamie said, shaking his head as he picked it up. "A lot of good it would have done me over here."

"Maybe we should head back to camp."

He nodded. "That's about all the excitement I can take in one morning anyway."

We hurried through the forest, looking over our shoulders frequently.

"Glad that bear wasn't a mama with cubs," Jamie said. "She would've torn us to shreds."

At the cabin he emptied his mushrooms into a bucket. We could hear Donnie and Will talking as they headed back for lunch.

"Don't tell them about the bear," Jamie whispered.

The three made sandwiches and sat around the truck eating.

"Too bad you didn't pick some mushrooms, Eric, so you could have a nice Vienna sausage sandwich," Donnie said.

"Yeah," Will added, "nothing like good old Vienna sausage and white bread."

I patted my belly. "That's all right. I'm so full of berries I don't believe I could eat a thing."

Donnie scowled at Jamie. "You let him pick berries?"

"How could I stop him? It's public land," Jamie said. "Besides, I was busy."

"Busy doing what?" Will sneered.

"Busy chasing away a bear, that's what!"

"Yeah, right." Will and Donnie snickered.

"It's true," I said.

They quit laughing. "You guys saw a bear?" Donnie said. "Really?"

"Weally," Jamie said smugly.

"Okay, tell us about it, birdbrain!"

"Ewic was picking bewwies when all of a sudden a giant gwizzly bear wose up out of the bushes. He must have been ten feet tall, don't you think, Ewic? He came charging wight at us."

"Did you shoot?" Donnie asked.

"I didn't want to hurt the bear if it wasn't necessawy. I just held my gun and waited. He came closer and closer. Thirty feet. Twenty feet. Ten feet. Then I said, 'Halt, bear!' And he stopped."

"You're lying," Will said.

"I stared that bear wight in the eye and told him to get out of here and don't ever come back. Tell them what the bear did, Ewic."

I cleared my throat. "The bear took off running across the tundra," I said, knowing at least I had told the truth.

"Lies, lies, lies," Will said, munching a cookie.

"Wait a minute," Donnie said. "Eric, is Jamie telling the truth?"

"We really did see a bear, and he ran off, " I replied.

"See there? And you made fun of me for bwinging the gun," Jamie said.

"Maybe we should all stick together this afternoon," Will said, pulling his little box of floss from his pocket and attacking his teeth with the thin green thread.

"Well, if you're afwaid," Jamie said, "I don't mind pwotecting you."

"Protecting us!" Donnie said. "I don't believe you could hit a bear with that gun if you tried."

"Well, I like to wait till I see the whites of their eyes," Jamie said. "I like to give the bear a fair chance."

18

That afternoon I stayed at the cabin while Jamie, Donnie, and Will went to pick mushrooms. They realized now that I wasn't going to pick any, so there wasn't much point in my going.

It didn't take me long, though, to begin to wish that I had walked along with them—at least it would have been half-way interesting. It took me all of about fifteen minutes to get bored with just sitting looking at the scenery, and I started looking around for something to do. And I found it in the back of the pickup—fishing gear! I chose a rod and tackle box and walked down to the water's edge, trying to remember what Mr. Bull had taught me about fishing. Trout fishing was different than salmon fishing, I knew. I needed a lightweight fly that floated on top of the water.

Opening the box, I picked out a nice yellow and black fly and tied it to the end of my line. Then I cast—but the fly swept in a crazy circle and caught the seat of my pants! I freed it and tried again. This time it landed in the water, but only a few inches from shore.

After several more tries I began to get the hang of it. I wasn't sure I was doing it right, but at least I was getting the fly out where a fish might be lurking.

After plenty of casts and no strikes, I moved down the shore looking for a better place. I climbed up onto a boulder that stuck out in the water, cast out into a deep pool—and immediately a fish struck hard, splashing as it grabbed the fly from the surface, and then dove. I began pulling it in, not too fast or the line might break. The fish felt heavy, but not as heavy as those salmon.

I tugged it slowly toward me, looking for the best place on the rock to pull it up. But *then* what would I do with it? I suddenly realized I had nowhere to put it!

When the fish was just a few feet from shore, I lay the rod down, wedging it against a rock, and sprinted to the truck. I found an empty bucket and raced back to my rock. Dipping the bucket full of water, I set it down and reached for my rod—only to find the line slack. Pulling up the empty hook, I groaned.

"I don't believe this," I muttered.

I decided to change flies, since this one looked ragged. As I was tying a new one on I suddenly realized that the buzzing sound I'd been hearing for the past minute or so was an airplane. I looked up quickly, and saw a small plane just a half-mile or so away. I watched it, wondering whether I should signal somehow to the pilot—and then the tip of the hook pricked my finger.

"Ow!" I said, looking down and checking the damage. Just a little spot of blood. I put my finger in my mouth and looked back up just in time to see the plane disappear behind a hillside.

I shrugged. Probably wouldn't have done me any good to signal, anyway. I finished tying the fly. "I'm going to get you this time, fish," I said softly.

I cast several times without luck. *The trout must be spooked*, I figured. I needed to find another place like this one. Scanning the shoreline, I saw another boulder not far away. Grabbing bucket and tackle box, I jumped to the ground and jogged toward it.

Tiptoeing onto the flat boulder, I threw the lure out, letting it touch the water ever so gently.

Whoosh! A fish sucked it down and disappeared. I couldn't believe my luck! This one seemed heavier than the last. I tried to pull in the line but the fish fought hard. Suddenly it leaped out of the water, a big, beautiful, shiny trout. It shook its head in midair, trying to throw the hook off, but no way; I'd hooked it good. It flopped back into the water, and I started bringing it in. Soon I could see the silvery creature in the clear water just a few feet from shore.

I walked backward, holding the line taut, and the trout came out of the water and lay flopping and sighing on the rock.

All right!

I got a grip on the slippery, struggling trout, unhooked the fly, and dropped the fish into the bucket of water. It thrashed fiercely, but couldn't get out.

I had just caught my own supper!

I jumped back onto the rock, hoping to catch another, and cast again.

Before the afternoon was over I'd landed three nice trout. I'd hooked a fourth one, too, but it got away. Proudly I lugged the heavy bucket back to the truck.

The guys weren't back yet. Good. Quickly I rustled up some wood and got a small campfire going. Then I cleaned the fish at the water's edge, like Mr. Bull had shown me. When I returned to the fire it had burned down to a nice bed of coals.

I'd read a book once about Blackfoot Indians in the Rocky Mountains, and I remembered how they cooked their fish. I laid the three trout side by side on the coals. Then I sat back to wait.

In ten minutes I turned them over. The once-shiny skin looked charred and leathery. But if the book was true, the flesh under it would be properly cooked.

"Well, the boy's got a fire going," said Donnie as the three men showed up, their bags half full.

"What's that he's cooking? Fish!" Jamie exclaimed.

I grinned. "Care to join me for supper? I've only got three but I'm sure we can share."

They stared at the fish, then at each other.

"But you're burning them," Donnie said.

"Oh, I don't think so. In fact, I think they should be just about ready." I pulled one onto a flat rock. Then I peeled back the blackened skin to reveal steaming white meat.

"Where are those fly rods?" Donnie said, hurrying to the truck. "I'm fish-hungry."

"Me too," said Will, joining him. "Maybe we can catch some for supper too."

"Yeah!" Jamie said. "And eat something instead of those old Vienna sausages for a change."

I smiled and took a bite of tender, delicious fish as the three men dashed to the lake, fishing rods in hand.

19

I was chewing my last bite of fish when I heard a shout from the lake. It sounded like Donnie. I expected he'd landed a big one, but then he added, "I'm hooked!"

"Just pull it out!" Jamie called.

"You guys be quiet. You'll spook the fish," Will muttered.

Donnie ignored him, moaning loudly as he came back toward camp.

"Cut this line for me, will you, Eric?" He held the rod in his right hand. The hook was deeply embedded in his left middle finger.

I pulled out my Swiss army knife and quickly cut the line. Donnie dropped the rod and held his finger close to his face, studying it.

"Man, this is in deep." He groaned. "I think I need to go to a doctor."

"Doctor?" Jamie frowned as he joined us. "There's no doctor within fifty miles. Here, let me see." He examined the finger. "Man! How'd you do it?"

"The line hung and when it came free it whizzed right into my finger," Donnie whined.

"Can't you just yank it out?" Jamie asked.

"Are you crazy?" Donnie said. "It's way past the barb."

"I got one!" Will called, thrashing his rod back and forth at the lake's edge. "I got a fish! Oh, darn, it got off."

"Will you knock it off?" Donnie yelled. "I got to get to a doctor."

Will trudged back toward us, looking disgusted. He stared at Donnie's finger. "Just pull it out. That hook's not very big."

"I can see you guys have never been hooked," Donnie said, cradling his hurt hand in the other. "I can't just pull it out. It'll rip my finger open."

"Hey," Jamie said. "I wemember weading an article in my outdoor magazine about how to wemove a fish hook."

"How?" Donnie asked, as if he were afraid to hear the answer.

"I'm twying to think." Jamie frowned. "I think you tie a line in the curve of the hook . . . No, maybe you tie it to . . . Oh, I'm sowwyy, Donnie, I just can't wemember. Seems like it was weal complicated."

"Wait a minute," I said. "I remember hearing about another way to get a hook out. It may hurt some, though."

"Don't like the sound of that much," Donnie said.

"A friend of mine told me about it. He got hooked and this is what his dad did. Actually, I think he said it didn't hurt that much after all."

"So tell me," Donnie said.

"Let me see your finger."

Reluctantly, he held out his long, skinny finger with the small, furry fly hanging from it.

"You take the hook and push it on through so the barb pops out your finger."

Donnie pulled his finger back. "Are you crazy?"

"Then you cut the barb off and pull the hook back out the way it came."

"No way am I going to push the hook through," Donnie said.

"But look, it's almost through already," I said, running my finger lightly over his skin and feeling the slight bulge of the barb.

Donnie felt it himself. "You're right."

"Maybe if you did it fast it wouldn't hurt so bad," Jamie suggested. "You know, like pulling off a bandaid."

"Gee, thanks," Donnie said sarcastically. "Getting a hook out of your finger is not like pulling off a bandaid."

"What do we cut the barb off with when he pushes it through?" Will asked with scientific curiosity.

"Got any pliers?" I asked.

"In the twuck," Jamie said. "I'll get them."

Donnie, meanwhile, was working up the courage to push the hook through. He squinched up his face as he grasped the metal eyelet.

"Hurry up with those pliers!" he shouted. "I'm going to do it!"

"Do it, then," Will grumbled. "My gosh."

Donnie took a deep breath and pushed. The sharp, tiny point of the hook poked through his finger, releasing a stream of bright red blood.

"Where are those pliers!" he yelled, grimacing.

Jamie jogged over, holding a pair of fat, grease-smeared pliers.

"You dummy!" Donnie groaned. "Those are too big!"

"Are you sure?" Jamie asked.

"Yes, I'm sure! Somebody find something, quick."

Jamie dashed to the truck, with Will behind him. Donnie held his hand up, his finger dripping blood, his face contorted with pain.

"Hey, I've got an idea," I said, taking my Swiss Army knife from my pocket. I pulled out the little scissors. "I wonder if this will cut metal."

"Try it, try it," Donnie said, offering me his finger.

I slipped the scissors under the barb and squeezed. Fortunately, the hook was tiny, and the thin wire gave. The barbed tip fell to the ground. Donnie carefully slid the rest of the hook out and put his finger in his mouth.

"'onk 'u," he grunted.

"You're welcome."

Just then Will and Donnie raced up. "Only thing we could find," Will said, holding up a hacksaw.

"Idiots!" Donnie said, removing his finger from his mouth. "Eric here already saved me."

I showed them my scissors.

"All wight, Ewic!" Jamie said, pulling my cap brim over my eyes playfully.

"Smart thinking, kid," Will chuckled. "I think Donnie here owes you his life."

Donnie put his uninjured hand around my shoulders and squeezed. "You're all right, you know that, Eric? Now, has anybody got any medicine to put on this?"

20

Later that night—though with the sun up it didn't seem like night at all—we heard an engine approaching. Soon Paul's jeep bounced out of the trees and skidded to a stop near the cabin. Paul jumped out with a scowl on his face.

"What's the matter, Paul?" Jamie said as the big man entered the cabin where we had candles burning.

"Bull's back, madder'n a hornet," Paul said in his high-pitched voice, shaking his head. "Accused me of lying and I said, 'Hey, I just confused you with somebody else.' But he knows something's up."

"Maybe we ought to move out of the park right now," Donnie said, stretched out on his sleeping bag.

Paul sat down in a small wooden chair that creaked under his weight. "That ain't all. Turns out this kid here has been lying to us all along." He pointed his finger at me. "He wasn't the only one up on Bear Ridge. There were two more!"

Jamie, sitting cross-legged on the floor near me, stared at me, hurt. "Why'd you lie to us, Ewic?"

"I didn't lie," I said, shaking my head. "I never said I was the only one up there. Nobody asked me."

"Well, Bull asked me about the kids and I said, 'What kids?'" Paul continued. "And he said, 'Sockeye Charlie—I told you to call him on the radio,' and I said, 'I tried. Couldn't get an answer.' I figured that was safe, since there wasn't any way he could find out I'd called this kid down off the mountain. But then he hauls out his radio and calls somebody and gets an answer! Turns out there's two other kids up there, and they told him about the call they got and that Eric here's missing. He told the other two to come on down. Then he really tears into me, threatening me with all kinds of things if I don't come up with Eric. I told him I just sell gas and run the lodge. I don't know anything about any kids, never got through to Sockeye Charlie, don't know any Eric and wish he'd just leave me alone."

The four of them just sat quietly for a minute or two, looking worried. "What are we going to do now?" Will fretted, lying on his side on his sleeping bag with his head propped in his hand.

"How's the picking going?"

"Good," Jamie said. "Especially near the base of that big hill to the west."

"Tell you what," Paul said. "Go ahead and collect all you can tomorrow morning. I'll be here around noon, take the mushrooms off your hands, then you guys can go on back to Anchorage."

"I don't like it," Will muttered. "What if Bull follows you?"

Paul scowled. "You think I wouldn't know if somebody was following me?"

"What about Ewic here?" Jamie asked.

Paul glared at me. "I been thinking about that. Can't just turn him over to Bull now. Things are getting so hot around here lately I've been thinking about delivering this batch of mushrooms to Tokyo myself. Maybe I'll just take Mr. Busybody here with me."

Jamie's eyes popped open wide. "What're you talking about? You'd kidnap Ewic and go all the way to Tokyo just to get out of a little fine? And what about us, left behind here?"

"It's you I'm thinking of," Paul said. "If I leave Eric behind here, he'll finger you for sure."

The three guys looked at each other, frowning. "What'll you do with Eric in Tokyo?" Donnie asked.

Paul shrugged. "Hey, if a kid should get lost in the back alleys of Tokyo or Hong Kong, who'd know the difference? Well, I'm out of here. See you guys tomorrow." He filled the doorway as he left. We heard the jeep crank up and drive off.

Jamie was the first to break the silence. "I don't like this. Ewic hasn't done anything."

"I don't like it either," Will said, after a pause, "but I don't know what we can do about it."

"Maybe we could take Ewic back to the lodge, let him go," Jamie said.

All right, Jamie, I thought.

But Will shook his head. "We let Eric go, we're gonna make Paul plenty mad—and if he calls in the loans he made us, we lose our business," Will said.

"Hey—do I need to point out that I could lose something here, too—like my life?" I said quietly. But they all three sat without saying anything.

Will and Jamie both looked at Donnie, but he just stared into space. Finally he mumbled, "Sorry, Eric, but Will's right. We've got to let Paul do what he thinks is best. There's just nothing we can do."

Jamie looked from Donnie to Will and from Will to Donnie, but neither of them said anything else. Finally he just looked down, sadly picking at his boots.

I couldn't believe it. Were these the same three guys I'd shared the past few days with? I jumped up and spat out, "Gee, thanks—pals." Disgusted, I walked outside.

Maybe I should run for it. Which was worse, being lost in the Alaskan wilderness or in the alleys of some Oriental city? As if to answer my question, a cold wind flung sharp, icy sleet at my face. And this was summertime? Between the bears and the weather and the endless miles of wilderness, I'd never make it out of here alive.

I was cold and wet, but I wasn't about to go back into a cabin full of traitors. I climbed into the cab of the pickup truck. Someone had left a down coat on the seat. I stretched out and pulled it over me. The nylon felt cold at first, but soon warmed me up.

Until now, being a prisoner of these guys hadn't seemed so bad. Yes, they were breaking the law, but I felt they were more victims of Paul's evil ways than anything else. Boy, had I been wrong —they were as bad as he was! All those warm feelings were gone now, for sure. Maybe they didn't want to hurt me themselves—but they were willing to sit back and let me be destroyed just to save their own necks.

Paul. He was something else. The other three would never have come up with any of this on their own. It had been his idea to kidnap me. He was blackmailing them to collect mushrooms for him. Now he was planning to take me off to Tokyo. And he probably wouldn't be content with just letting me get lost. He'd rather make a profit off me. He'd probably sell me into slavery!

Now that I was by myself, I couldn't hold the tears back any longer, and I groaned in misery.

The wind answered, howling outside the truck. Sleety rain tapped the windshield.

I felt like a failure. What was it Miss Spice had said? *I just wish there was some way to educate people so they wouldn't do these things to start with.* Well, sorry, Miss Spice, but there isn't.

And Sharon had said something about Christians making people better. Hate to break it to you, Sharon, but these guys are getting worse, not better. They're about to send me into slavery in Japan.

I shivered and pulled the coat tighter around my neck.

Mr. Bull was right. These people were nothing but thugs and lowlifes.

21

When I woke, the morning sun shone wetly through the windshield. I climbed out of the truck and stretched in the brisk air. The clean blue sky was flecked with high clouds, like stone-washed denim.

"Jamie? Will? Donnie?" I peeked inside the cabin. Empty. The guys must have gotten an early start, since this was their last chance to pick mushrooms here.

Hungry, I headed for the nearest berry patch. This might be my last chance to eat anything other than chow mein!

But the berries didn't seem very filling; as I popped one after another into my mouth and munched, I kept

thinking about how good the trout tasted last night. So I grabbed the rod, bucket, and tackle box. Maybe I could catch one of those that got away.

As I fished, the brisk, clear weather made all my fears of the night before seem less real. Maybe I *could* make it back down to the lodge. It would probably be a three-or-four-day hike, but if I stayed close to the road—not right on it, of course, or Paul and the others would find me—I shouldn't get lost. And there'd be berries to eat, and fish, too, if I took a rod along with me.

Right now the fish weren't biting. Maybe the changing weather had given them lockjaw. I was thinking about moving farther down the lake when I heard a branch crack.

Turning, I saw a mama bear and two cubs, just yards away, coming right toward me! And what scrawny, skinny, mangy-looking bears! They looked like they were starving, diseased or both.

There was nowhere to run, nowhere but the lake itself—and bears could swim. This was it. It was all over.

Eric Sterling, killed at age twelve by attacking grizzlies! Even if I survived the attack I'd probably get rabies.

I turned and was about to jump into the lake when a muffled voice said, "Wait, Eric C.!"

Wait, when bears were about to attack? And who was talking? I looked over my shoulder; the bears had stopped. One of the cubs reached up with its paws, grabbed the sides of its head, and looked like it was trying to pull its head off. Then, to my amazement, it *did* pull its head off—and it was Erik K., in bear costume! The other two bears pulled their heads off too, revealing Sharon and Mr. Bull. No wonder they looked puny.

My knees felt weak as fishing line, and I sat down hard on the rock so that I wouldn't fall. My head spun. The fear had been so intense that now I thought I was going to pass out.

"You okay, big guy?" Erik K. said, waddling toward me, his legs hobbled by the short back legs of the bear suit.

Despite my fear, Erik's funny walk cracked me up. Sharon laughed too. Mr. Bull patted my back.

"Didn't mean to scare you so bad, Eric C . . . Thought about coming up with our heads off, but that might have been worse . . ." He chuckled. "Three bears with the heads of humans . . ."

We all laughed. I held my hands tight against me so no one would see that they were still trembling.

"So, are you going to make me *ask* why you're dressed up in bear suits?" I said.

Mr. Bull glanced around. "Where are those three men, anyway? Didn't see 'em at the cabin."

"Off picking mushrooms, I think," I said.

"Did you see us fly over yesterday?" Sharon asked. "We saw you."

Of course—the airplane that flew over while I was fishing. "Yeah! That was you guys?"

Mr. Bull nodded. "When I realized that Paul guy lied and you were missing . . . Knew something bad was happening . . . Figured you'd been kidnapped . . . Decided to do an air search . . ."

"And now you're going to arrest the guys?" I asked.

Mr. Bull nodded. "Park rangers due here soon for backup . . . First we want to scare a little sense into these guys . . ." He grinned through his bushy black beard. "Thought these bear outfits might do the trick . . . Park rangers had 'em, use 'em in skits for tourists . . ."

"Boy, they sure look real—even if they are kind of mangy," I said, touching the shaggy brown fur.

Erik looked around. "When do you think those three guys'll be back?"

"Noon at the latest."

"Any idea where they are now?" Mr. Bull asked.

"Jamie said something about the foot of the hill west of the lake." I pointed. "Over there, I guess."

"Tell you what," Mr. Bull said as we walked back toward the cabin—or as I walked and they waddled. "You go meet 'em . . . We'll hide here in the woods by the cabin . . . You start whistling when you come up so we know you're close . . . Then when you get here, we jump out, scare the guys' pants off . . . And the rangers come in and arrest 'em."

I nodded and tried to answer, but I just couldn't. The whole thing was too bizarre. Finally I leaned against a tree and burst out laughing.

"What's so funny about that?" Mr. Bull asked, but by that time Sharon and Erik K. were laughing, too.

"What's so *funny* about it?" I said. "This has got to be the weirdest bust in history! I mean, I feel like I'm in a cartoon or something."

"I should have a badge!" Erik K. choked out between laughs. "So I could hold it up and say, 'Bear police! Halt or I'll bite!'" He fell over and rolled in the pine needles.

"Guess it is pretty funny," Mr. Bull grinned, scratching his whiskers with the bear's three-inch claws. "But it oughta cure 'em, too . . . Three bears come charging up to 'em . . ."

"Three of the skinniest, mangiest bears they've ever seen!" I gasped, tears running down my cheeks.

"Scared *you*, didn't we?" Mr. Bull said.

I wiped my eyes and stopped laughing suddenly. "Uh-oh, wait a minute. Jamie has a gun."

Mr. Bull frowned. "Any chance you can unload it without him knowing, before you get back?"

"Maybe." I shrugged. "Or maybe not."

"Tell you what . . . If the gun's unloaded, whistle . . . If it's loaded, sing."

"Sing?"

"Sure," Erik K. said. "If you're whistling, it's safe."

"And if you're singing, it's not," finished Sharon.

"But what'll you do if I'm singing?" I asked.

"Then we wait," Mr. Bull said. "When Jamie sets his gun down, you sneak it out of the way . . . kick it under the truck or something . . ."

"Okay."

We stopped at the cabin and I put the fishing tackle in the bed of the pickup.

"We'll be hiding in the woods," Mr. Bull said.

"Hey, where's your van?" I asked.

"Hid it back up the road."

Erik K. rubbed his paws together. "Boy, this is gonna be fun!"

"Be careful, Eric C.," Sharon said as I turned to go.

I grinned and gave her a thumbs up. She probably would have given me one back if she'd had any thumbs. I took one last look at my funny-looking friends, shook my head, and set off to find the mushroom smugglers.

22

I spotted Donnie's tall blue form and Will's short red one through the woods. But where was Jamie? Then I saw a tall clump of bushes shaking. So he was picking berries! That meant he had probably set his gun down somewhere nearby. If only I could get to it and unload it without him knowing.

Remembering the Blackfoot Indian book, I began to slip from tree to tree, staying out of sight of the men. When I neared the berry thicket, I dropped to all fours and began to creep. I could see Jamie's blue-jeaned legs and muddy boots as he plucked fruit, humming softly. He had no idea I was there. I tingled with excitement.

And there it was, the shotgun—lying on the ground several yards from Jamie. Perfect! Moving carefully and silently, I crept toward it, keeping an eye out for Jamie. My hands shook as I slowly reached for the gun, stretched out my fingers to wrap around it—and suddenly Jamie's voice startled me. I froze.

"Hey, guys!" he called, his mouth full. "I weally found a bunch of bewwies over here!"

"Quit eating and pick!" Donnie called back.

Swiftly I picked the gun up. But before I could unload it, Jamie's footsteps approached. I replaced the gun just in time and grabbed a handful of berries.

"Ewic! I didn't hear you come up." Jamie said.

"I got bored," I said, rising and tossing a berry in my mouth. "Thought I'd join you."

He frowned. "What were you doing down there?"

"Noticed you got something on your gun," I said, thinking fast. "Looks like water. See? You want to keep that dry or it'll rust."

"Oh, yeah. Thanks." He picked it up, brushed it off, and slung it over his shoulder.

That would probably be my last chance to unload the gun! I felt like punching something, I was so disappointed. But I tried to stay calm and stuck close to Jamie, just in case he set it down again.

"Okay, guys," Donnie said as we approached. "It's after eleven. Better be getting back." He looked up. "Oh, hey, Eric, I didn't know you were here."

"Thought I'd join you," I said.

"Lunchtime," Jamie said. "I'm hungwy."

"You're always hungry," Will teased, stepping out of a berry thicket. "If we took all the money you spent on food, we could have paid Paul off long ago."

We headed back toward the cabin.

"Find many mushrooms?" I asked.

"Mushrooms?" Will said, grinning as if he knew something I didn't know. "Who said anything about mushrooms?"

The other two grinned at me too. "Didn't pick mushroom one, Eric," Donnie said.

I didn't think they were funny. "Knock it off, guys. I know you've got something in your sacks."

Jamie grinned. "Bewwies." He put an arm on my shoulders. "We had a talk last night after you went out, Ewic. We decided you're wight about the mushwooms. And Paul is wong, definitely wong."

Donnie nodded. "We're not going to let him take you to Tokyo either," he added.

I stopped and stared at them in wonder. "Are you guys kidding me?"

They grinned. "We let ourselves be fooled by Paul," Will said, reaching into his sack and pulling out some berries, which he popped into his mouth. "But that's over. We're gonna find an honest way out of debt and quit breaking the law. Here, want some berries?"

"You bet!" I took a handful from his bag and we started walking again.

"Yeah," Donnie said. "We figured we might as well use this last morning to stock up on berries to take back to Anchorage."

"Wow, this is really great, guys," I told them proudly. "But what changed your minds?"

Donnie punched my arm playfully. "You did, Eric. What you said made sense, for one thing, even though we didn't want to admit it. But besides that, you've been good to us no matter how mean we were to you."

Ooops. Instant guilt trip. *Better catch the lawbreakers and throw 'em in jail, that's what I say,* I had told Sharon and Miss Spice, when they'd said that Christians ought to try to change people for the better. I had agreed with Mr. Bull, when he'd said these people were nothing but crooks and lowlifes. Now the "crooks and lowlifes" were real people with real faces and real names.

The cabin! I suddenly realized that we were almost back to it, and Jamie's gun was still loaded! I'd been thinking so hard— I cleared my throat quickly, ignoring my half-chewed mouthful of berries, and began to sing: "Buffalo gals won't you come out tonight—" I took a quick breath—and inhaled a piece of berry. I coughed. It was stuck! I tried to sing: "Come out—" I choked and coughed.

"What are you doing, Ewic?" Jamie interrupted.

"He's singing," Donnie said. "I think. Either that or dying. Hard to tell."

"Come—" Nothing doing. I coughed again, hard, and finally got rid of the unchewed berry and spat it out. I gulped air and screeched at the top of my lungs, "Come out tonight!"

Too late! To my horror I saw three bears amble out of the woods. They must not have heard me in time! They began to waddle toward us.

"Bears!" Will shouted.

23

"Wun away! Wun away!" Jamie screamed. Dropping cap, gun, and sack, he headed toward the nearest tree. Will and Donnie also took off running.

Thank goodness Jamie hadn't thought to use his gun! Our plan would work after all. Now we just had to make sure Donnie, Jamie, and Will were good and scared.

"Help! Bears!" I shouted, trying to sound frightened. I decided to fall down and play dead. As I lay on my back, the three bears stopped just a few steps away.

"They're in the trees," I whispered. "See? Over there. You guys go over and scratch at the tree trunks."

But the larger cub ran over and jumped on top of me, wrestling playfully.

"Knock it off, Erik!" I whispered furiously. "Go scare those guys."

Without answering he leaned down and licked my face with a hot, wet, scratchy tongue.

Wait a minute. Bear suits didn't come with hot, wet, scratchy tongues!

"Eric! Look out! Those are real bears!"

Craning my neck, I saw Mr. Bull, Erik K. and Sharon standing helplessly near the cabin, holding their costume heads in their hands.

All the blood seemed to drain from my body, and all my strength with it. I wanted to throw this cub off my chest and run for a tree, but I barely had strength to breathe. This was for real! I was *really* done for this time!

The real mama bear had spun around angrily at the sound of my friends' voices, and now with a fierce grunt she charged the three fake, headless bears, who turned and ran for the cabin. They raced inside and slammed the door behind them just in time. The big mama grizzly slammed into the door with such force I'm surprised the whole cabin didn't fall over, then she clawed at it and growled ferociously.

"Play dead, Ewic," Jamie coached from a nearby treetop.

"Yeah," said Donnie from another tree. "She won't bother you if you play dead."

117

The cub licked my face again, and the other cub wandered over, sniffing my ear. Its bristles tickled, and I couldn't help but giggle. Both cubs began licking my face, neck and ears, and I giggled again, panicking.

"Shhh! Be quiet, Ewic!" Jamie said.

I tried. Oh, how I tried. But their rough tongues tickled!

"Look out, here comes the mother!" Donnie said.

I heard heavy footsteps. That did it; I stopped giggling. I stopped breathing. I stopped *everything*, absolutely paralyzed. Closing my eyes, I felt the shadow of the huge grizzly fall across me. The cubs quit licking and climbed off. I heard the breathing of the mother bear as she leaned over to inspect me. Her hot breath blew across my face, and I trembled as her cold, wet nose brushed across my chin. She grunted once, as if to say I wasn't worth bothering with, then she and the cubs lumbered away. Opening my eyes, I saw them disappear into the forest.

For a long time I lay completely still. Nobody else moved either. We were all afraid the bears would return. The wind sighed in the spruce trees. A fly buzzed around my face. Bees hummed among flowers nearby.

When I heard an approaching motor, I raised my head. A pale green jeep roared up to the cabin and screeched to a stop. The doors swung open and two rangers jumped out, guns drawn. One held a megaphone to his mouth.

"Everyone come out with your hands up! You're under arrest for the illegal harvesting of protected mushrooms!" The voice boomed through the forest.

Slowly the cabin door opened and three bears with human heads walked out, their paws in the air.

The two rangers gaped in surprise. Then the younger one turned to the older one and said, "You ever run into this situation before, Frank? What do we do now?"

"We're not the smugglers, you idiots," Mr. Bull growled. He turned and spotted Will, Donnie, and Jamie, clinging to tree limbs. Mr. Bull pointed with his paw. "Over there. Up in the trees."

The rangers wheeled around. "Come down from those trees with your hands up!" boomed the megaphone.

"How can we climb down a tree with our hands up?" muttered Donnie as they made their way down the trunks.

Still shaky, I slowly got up and dusted myself off, my face sticky from bear tongues. Sharon, Erik, and Mr. Bull hurried to my side.

"Are you all right?" Sharon asked.

"Man, I thought you were done for!" Erik K. said.

Mr. Bull examined my face. "Few scratches . . . Those bears have rough tongues, no doubt about it . . ."

I looked up. The rangers had already handcuffed Donnie, Will, and Jamie and were leading them toward the jeep.

"Wait a minute!" I said. "Officers, those guys aren't the real smugglers. It's that other guy, Paul. He's the one who kidnapped me, and he's black-mailing these guys to make them pick mushrooms."

The older ranger, Frank, who had short black hair and wore sunglasses, said, "Paul? You mean Paul Rico, the guy who runs Bear Lodge?"

"That's wight!" Jamie said.

"And he's due here at noon," Donnie added.

The rangers glanced at Mr. Bull, who combed his beard with a paw. "People, we need to come up with a plan . . ."

24

Erik K., Sharon, and I peered through a big crack in the cabin wall. Erik held a video camera, one that Mr. Bull kept in his van for filming wildlife.

"Are you sure you know how to work that?" she asked her brother.

"Yep. It's a cinch!"

"I hope they're careful," Sharon said as we stared out at Jamie, Donnie, and Will, who sat on the tailgate of their pickup. Behind them I could just make out the form of a grizzly bear—Mr. Bull, that is, playing dead in the back of the truck.

"Don't worry. This'll work great," Erik reassured his sister. "Paul won't suspect a thing. Mr. Bull's van is hidden, and the rangers hid their jeep."

"He does have a pistol, though," I pointed out.

"Yeah, but so do the rangers, and they're hiding right over there in the woods," Erik K. said.

"Listen!" Sharon said. "A motor."

Soon we heard the rumble of a vehicle, and Paul's jeep bounced out of the forest and skidded to a stop. Erik began filming through the crack as Paul climbed out and walked over to the three guys. We just could hear his voice.

"Well, you guys do any good this morning?" he asked. "Hey, what—a bear!"

Jamie grinned. "Good thing I cawwy that shotgun, isn't it, Paul? That bear attacked us when we were walking back to the cabin."

"Are you guys crazy?" he said, leaning over to inspect the animal. "Don't you know it's against the law to kill a grizzly?"

"It's against the law to pick mushrooms, too," Will pointed out.

"Yeah, but you can hide mushrooms. What are you going to do with this thing?"

"Maybe we could eat it," Donnie said.

"Or sell the hide," Will added.

"Or you could stuff it and put it at your lodge," Jamie offered.

"No way! You guys do what you want with it, but keep it away from my lodge. I've got enough trouble with the law as it is. Man, that's one ugly bear. Well, let me see what you got."

The men emptied yesterday's pickings on the tail-gate.

"Not bad," Paul said, examining the crop. "I'll get a good price for these in Tokyo. Say, where's the kid?"

"In the cabin," Will said.

"All right. Well, look, I'll pay you something to cover expenses, and then I'll take the kid with me. I know a place I can stash him till I get ready to leave the country." He pulled out his wallet.

"You getting all this on film?" I whispered to Erik.

"Shhh. Yes."

Paul handed each of the men some bills.

"Hey, when are we going to get out of debt to you, anyway?" Jamie asked.

"Soon, boys, soon. Another season or two of picking and we'll call it even."

As he swept the mushrooms into a bucket, an odd grunt came from the back of the truck.

"What was that?" Paul said.

"What was what?" Donnie said.

Another grunt sounded, louder.

"Hey! That bear's not dead!" Paul hissed, staring at the shaggy mound.

"*Got* to be dead," Jamie said. "I shot him right in the heart."

The bear twitched.

"Where's your gun?" Paul said urgently. "You better put another load of lead into that thing."

Suddenly the bear roared to life. Jamie, Donnie, and Will scattered and Paul staggered back as the bear rose up in the back of the pickup truck, looked around, and leaped to the ground. With a growl, the bear charged. Paul tripped and fell flat on his back as the beast climbed on top of him.

"Help! Somebody do something! He's killing me!" Paul screamed.

But Donnie, Jamie, and Will gathered around him, laughing hilariously.

"Are you guys crazy?" Paul shouted. "I could die here!"

But the bear stood up, reached up with its paws and pulled its head off. Mr. Bull stared at Paul with a grin.

"What the—" Paul stammered.

The two rangers appeared behind Mr. Bull, guns drawn. One unsnapped a pair of handcuffs. "You're under arrest for mushroom smuggling."

Paul sat up slowly, still breathing hard and sweating. "You got no proof," he protested weakly.

"Oh yes we do," said Erik K. as we stepped out of the cabin with the video camera.

Paul pointed a finger at the three mushroom pickers. "Well, if I go to jail, you guys are going with me!"

"I wouldn't be so sure of that," Mr. Bull said. "Ever hear of a law against blackmail? As I recall, you admitted making them pick mushrooms because they owe you money . . ."

"They still broke the law!"

"That's true. But I'll bet the judge will take into consideration that you forced them to break it . . . Especially if they testify against you . . ."

Paul covered his face with his hands and groaned.

25

"Boy, have we got a surprise for you," I said to Miss Spice as Erik K., Sharon, and I trooped up to her desk.

"What is it?" she asked.

"You're gonna love it," I said.

"Are you going to tell me what it is, or make me guess?" she said with a laugh.

From behind his back Erik pulled a plastic case about three feet long. We grinned at Miss Spice's puzzled expression. "What . . ."

"Unscrew the top," Sharon said.

Miss Spice unscrewed it and pulled out a fly rod, broken down into two pieces. "A fishing pole!"

"Not just a fishing pole, Miss Spice," Erik said, helping her assemble it. "A fly rod. You can catch salmon and trout on it."

"And Mr. Bull said you can even catch bream and bass," Sharon added.

"Oh, there's plenty of those around here," Miss Spice said. "This is so sweet of you kids. Thank you."

She came around her desk and gave each of us a kiss on the cheek. Then she returned to her chair. We sat down too.

"I can't wait to use this," she said.

"We'll show you how," I said. "We're practically experts by now."

"I believe it!" Miss Spice said. "You're also experts in catching mushroom smugglers. The Denali Park rangers called me again today to thank me for sending you three up there. It turns out that Paul Rico was responsible for most of the mushroom smuggling in the park. The three men you met weren't the only ones he was blackmailing. He had lots of collectors working for him, usually against their will. Thanks to you kids, practically the entire Alaskan mushroom smuggling business has come to a halt."

"All right!" Erik K. said, pumping his fist.

"What about Jamie and Donnie and Will?" I asked. "They won't go to jail, will they?"

Miss Spice shook her head. "No, they won't, and you're partly responsible for that, Eric C. They said you convinced them they'd been damaging the park by picking mushrooms, and they want to do whatever they can to make up for it. That means not only testifying against Rico, but also helping stock Denali National Park with mushrooms again."

"That's great!" Sharon said.

Miss Spice smiled, then wrinkled her forehead in an expression of concern. "How did you children get along with Mr. Bull, by the way?"

"He's cool," Erik K. said, and I nodded.

"He's sweet," Sharon added. "I miss him."

"That's funny. Some people tell me he's extremely rude," Miss Spice said.

The three of us looked at each other and grinned. "Well, that's true too," I said.

"Yeah," Sharon said. "Sometimes he can really be a bear, know what I mean?"

Miss Spice just shook her head and smiled as we burst into laughter.